P9-DCS-459

ANDREW J. OFFUTT

VOLUME TWO OF

WAR OF THE GODS ON EARTH

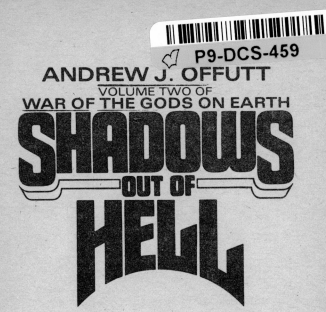

SHADOWS

OUT OF

HELL

A BERKLEY BOOK
published by
BERKLEY PUBLISHING CORPORATION

SHADOWS OUT OF HELL

A Berkley Book / published by arrangement with
the author

PRINTING HISTORY
Berkley edition / February 1980

ISBN: 0-425-04447-5

A BERKLEY BOOK® TM 757,375
PRINTED IN THE UNITED STATES OF AMERICA

THE SWORD OF
THE IRON LORDS

"They are dead."

"All three? You slew them all three?"

"Yes, I alone!" Jarik cried. "The Black Sword and I were one. My mind had fled. I fight *morbin*, Kirrensark. I don't think. I just fight and when it is done I awake, and wonder at my prowess!"

SHADOWS OUT OF HELL
VOLUME TWO OF
WAR OF THE GODS ON EARTH

Andrew J. Offutt

*Titles in the WAR OF THE GODS ON EARTH series
by Andrew J. Offutt*

THE IRON LORDS
*SHADOWS OUT OF HELL

*Published by Berkley Publishing Corporation

SHADOWS OUT OF HELL

All across the broad earth
  dark shadows sprawl;
Sent forth from the Iron Lords
  and Snowmist's hall.

Like shadows out of Hell
  they lord over all—
Even to Osyr's fair isle
  their shadows fall.

Jarik his name, of the Black Sword
  a warrior tall—
The Man who was Two Men
  ever under a pall.

From the keep of Iron Lords
  at Snowmist's call;
Like shadows out of hell
  hold him in thrall.

Contents

There were gods on the earth in those days, and there was strife among them.

It was humankind they fought over, and its future on the earth, and humans fought in that war the gods came to wage among themselves. First among those warriors of humankind was Jarik who was two men, and who wielded the black sword of god-metal he had of the Iron Lords.

And this is one of the stories of the war among the gods on the earth, and how Jilain Kerosyris came into it, called also Zhilain and Yilain.

"You are a Mystery on the earth, Jarik. A very, very central pawn. Neither do the Iron Lords your masters know who you are, Jarik—and they have some fear of you."

—The Lady of the Snowmist

1

Asea Without a Helmsman

"The Lady of the Snowmist is pure evil, Jarik: reddest, ineffable evil. She is dedicated to ridding this world of men as we know them, to be replaced by...something else."

—The Iron Lords

"Poor Jarik! You are but a rusty hoe in the hands of a stout farmer! A tool, Jarik. The Iron Lords could not suffer you to live, nor are you the sort of tool they would merely hang up in a place of honor on the shed wall. You would be less than an ant beneath their world-stamping feet!"

—The Lady of the Snowmist

"It is impossible that contrary attributes should belong at the same time to the same subject."

—Aristotle

A stout gusty wind hurried the ship along under striped sail. The sea gurgled past her flanks in hedges of blued green flecked with white blossoms. The sail did not snap but strained at its stays, standing forth like the belly of a gravid woman. Spindrift sprang across the larboard gunwale in a spray of cloud and crystal. If any man minded, he said nothing.

Twice a man's height the ship was at the waist. Some eight man-lengths separated the carven hawk's head at the prow from the stern, which lofted upward arrogant as the tail of a feisty cock. Light as a champion games-runner, she ran over the waves. Every man aboard was accustomed now to the little bounce-bounce-bounce. None took note or was jarred. Spray slopped into a bailing well with no scupper for returning sea to sea. Now and again men must bail. Over that plain of green and blue spattered with spumey flashes of white, the ship called *Seadancer* fled like a teasing maiden in springtime.

Twoscore and two men rode her, and one was Jarik of the Black Sword, agent of the Iron Lords.

Gazing aloft Jarik said, "Her gull never veers or strays, but flies like a hurled spear."

"We have only to follow," Kirrensark said, and he shrugged massive round shoulders.

No man needed to take notched stick and hold it out as far as he could stretch his arm, squinting while he stared at the place where sea and sky became skysea. No one need take note of the sun at all, or of the stars. The gull led them. The only man who strove was he who presently held the steering-oar. He sat to rightward of the stern, on the steer-board side. Even his task was dull, and the men of *Seadancer* took short turns.

"It hardly flaps a wing," Jarik said, sounding not wondering but sad. A bit wistful, perhaps. Nor did he look at the big man beside him in the bow, master of Kirrensark-wark and of *Seadancer*.

"No. A bird of sorcery. And what are we to expect, we mere men? We are but to follow, to take you where the gull leads us. It is the servant of Her."

"As I am," Jarik said, and this time he was definitely morose. He repeated, almost inaudibly, "As I am."

Kirrensark's one hand flexed open and shut, open and shut. He looked from the younger man's face to his wrist, where a long bracer gleamed as if just polished. Jarik's other forearm was identically circled and contained. The silvery cylinders might have been the ornaments they resembled, lengthened to afford protection and add strength to the thick wrists of a man of weapons. Ornamental bracers, then.

They were not. Kirrensark knew it in wonder and Jarik knew it in bitterness.

They were bonds. The armlets bound him to Her, the god on the earth, by god-sorcery. He was silver-bound to the Lady of the Snowmist in her silver armor and mask.

Milady Snowmist, and the wark, and the shore of Lokusta lay far behind them.

"I came to Kirrensark-wark to slay Her," Jarik said tonelessly. "And now I am her servant. Her slave! I came to your wark to slay you—and now I am allied with you."

"After you saved my life," Kirrensark said, looking as if he wanted to touch the taller, slimmer man. He did not. Kirrensark knew that Jarik talked for himself as much as for his companion; that Jarik saw himself only as a figure of tragedy, a victim.

Jarik's head jerked in a sharp short nod. "Aye. After I saved your life." After a moment he added, "Had I known who was the one-armed man those three sought to slay, I'd have remained on that hill and merely watched."

Kirrensark knew that. He took it in silence, and went as pensive as Jarik.

Years ago, more than a decade but less than two decades ago, Kirrensark Long-haft had led strong men aboard a hawk-prowed ship and gone a-hawking. He did not know why. Milady Snowmist had told Jarik that it was because Kirrensark was then controlled by the Iron Lords. (What would they tell him, those Gods on the Earth who were surely her brothers?) He and his men had rowed and sailed far and far, to westward and south. They had come to land, a chalky cliff shining above the sea. There sprawled a farmers' community. With sword and ax the tall hawkers slew those peaceful people. Among the slain had been those Jarik called mother and father.

Kirrensark was sure they were not. With his wheaten

hair and those eyes like blued, polished iron, Jarik belonged among the people he now abode with. The people of Lokusta. The Lokustans of the northerly land lived without kings or lords, in their *warks* named for the firstman. They lived under the aegis of the Lady of the Snowmist, or of the Iron Lords. Gods on the Earth. The folk of the warks of Lokusta were fair of hair and blue or grey of eye and quick to go ruddy or freckled of skin pale as shadeflowers. And so Jarik. How could he be other than a Lokustan born?

Would that he were born of Lirushyé and Kirrensark, Kirrensark thought, *and thus my own son!*

As if he knew the channel in which Kirrensark's thoughts flowed twisting, Jarik said in that dull voice, "I was eight. My mother Thanamee was carrying my brother-to-be within her. His name would have been Oak."

"Oak?"

The short nod; Jarik was not looking at Kirrensark, who saw only the side of his face. That bony jaw might have been carved out with a hand-ax. "Oak. I wanted a brother. I had a sister. Torsy was less than a year older than I was. She had brown hair, sort of dark tawny like my father's. How I wanted a brother!"

"You never thought it might have been another sister."

Jarik turned his head and his eyes were hard as blued iron. "He'd have been a boy, a brother named Oak."

Kirrensark's hand worked at his side. He nodded, then looked away from the glacier-cold stare. He could not challenge Jarik. Jarik was young and swift and two-handed, and he was mighty in combat. More importantly he had saved the life of Kirrensark that afternoon two weeks ago when Kirrensark's own nephew and two others tried to murder him. None would make a better son-in-law than this Jarik of the Black Sword who had disdained Kirrensark's offer that his daughter Iklatne and Jarik go before the Lady Mage, to be wedded.

They were servants together of the god on the earth, and asea together in her service.

She was Kirrensark's god and his wark's protector, was the Lady of the Snowmist. He served Her more than willingly, though the sea air with its constant briny spray and pervading damp laid an ache in the stump of his arm. He felt an occasional needling pang in the fingers that were not there.

Jarik counted Her as enemy and served Her nonetheless. He had to. The seamless bracers, armbands of silver, saw to that. He had tried. Three days ago he had blurted of a sudden that they were far and far from Lokusta and he must be out of reach of her power. Jarik had tried. Every man aboard saw his pain. It did not begin and build; it was instantly egregious and unbearable. They saw it in his face and twitching body and they knew it emanated from the handsome armlets on his wrists. He served Snowmist! She saw to that. He was on mission for Her, and she held him to it. Like Kirrensark, like the gull, like Jarik, the bracers served Her from afar. They linked him to Her.

And the gull guided them. Grey with white and grey-white so that it was often silvery in the sunlight that dappled the water with white and silver.

"Slain," Jarik was saying, staring ahead as if there was aught to see. "All slain. My mother and my brother within her, and my father, and all the others. Slain. And Oceanside burned. My home, and all the homes."

Jarik went silent, his mouth a straight line as if slit there by a dagger. Kirrensark said nothing. He was no loquacious man anyhow; he was a leader. Neither was Jarik much for talking. Hearing him do so after their days and days asea was surprising. The sea must be bringing it back to him, Kirrensark thought. The sea, and riding beneath the striped sail of a hawk-prowed ship. It was Jarik's first time off land since... That Day. Though the words accused, and hurt, and his remembering was dangerous to the firstman of the Lokustan community or wark named for him, Kirrensark was fascinated to hear Jarik talk, and pleased.

Poor Jarik, he thought. Talk on. *Perhaps you will talk it out, lessen the gnawing hurt, poor boy so full of hate and hurt and bitterness.*

"Two survived," Jarik said. "Only two. Torsy, and Jarik. We had been sent to fish and were just returning. We were not there to be seen. All that could be seen were slain. Blood splashed like red spindrift. We survived. I saw, and Torsy saw, and we both lost our minds and fell down unconscious. She remained always...peculiar, Torsy did, and I—I have not healed, in the head. Oak is with me."

A strange remark, Kirrensark thought. An unborn child that might or might not have been a boy, might or might not have been named Oak. How the fairest haired among those people had wanted company! And still did! He had probably assumed that Oak, "Oak," would somehow be born with hair and eyes identical to Jarik's; his..."brother."

Oak is with me, he said now, as if there had been one called Oak.

"I was eight," Jarik said, staring at the sea ahead. "Eight! and next day I set out with her in a boat. A *boat*! I rowed. My hands blistered and popped and bled and I plunged them over the boat's side into the salt water and was embarrassed—mortified when that wrenched a groan from me. What agony that was! I was eight, and thought I had to be a man. I would have vengeance! I had vowed it. I would follow those killers from the sea and I would kill them all. I, Orrikson Jarik of Oceanside. Eight years old! Rowing a little boat. Falling asleep at night and probably drifting leagues and leagues...thinking I was following those murderers of my people—of my life!"

The cords of muscle swelled on his neck and the odor of brine filled the air. *Seadancer*'s wake slurped and gurgled like a greedy drinker of ale. *Seadancer* sailed over the sea drinking sea, and now and again men bailed. Though once he had offered Jarik his life, Kirrensark feared now that at any instant the young man would whirl on him, and do him violence.

Kirrensark hoped that he had the strength not to resist.

Somewhere ahead lay Kerosyr. The Isle of Osyr, the dead god. Their goal, for Her. The bird flew on. The wind remained behind them, impossibly keeping their sail bellied. *Seadancer* raced on, on a voyage weird and impossible. Only at night did the gull take rest, atop the ship's mast.

"We would have died, of course," Jarik said, and pain was lead in his voice. "We were saved instead. The ship that happened along had a huge ugly beaked head at its prow! It was not the same ship, but I fought those men. I hated all hawk-men, Lokustans. They rescued us anyhow. Hating, always an outsider, I grew up among them. In Ishparshule-wark, in the land of the Lords of Iron. I was small then, and I was different, from afar; and so they taunted me and Torsy and bullied me. I hated! I fought! I knew a new father and mother. They *were* mother and father to me, too. He saw how I fought—mindless, outside myself—and he began to train me to weapons. He loved them, though he had never had to fight. I became better than he. I became the best weaponer among them. Very late, long after all the others, I got my growth. I grew more than any! I wasn't short anymore or skinny either. But goaded, outcast!—sneered at, hating!—having proved myself again and again to no avail. One day I ... succumbed to goading. I slew. He was a year older than I, and his sword was in his hand. I was exiled. Some said I should be slain. Pride sent me forth with a straight back and angry words. I did not deny killing Stath; I denied *them*! And Torsy, poor Torsy who now I know was not my sister for I was truly no more of Oceanside than of Ishparshule-wark ... Torsy came with me. We were all right. We had always taken care of ourselves. We had always been alone, no matter how many were around us. We were all right," he said again, with a hard jerk of his head.

He surely exaggerates, Kirrensark mused. *For he did say that he was adopted, and that those foster-parents— second set of foster-parents!—were as parents to him. Bitterness and hate are crowned in him, and rule, so that he exaggerates.*

"Torsy and I fared through the woods and came to a shore. Within days I slew again, twice. Two men who sought to have her, on the beach where we tarried. Both were weaponers, in their prime. I slew both, and was not wounded. And I saw to Torsy. They had hurt her."

Bitterness drives him, Kirrensark reflected. And hurt ... and pride. The pride of him! Not even his failures, his misery, not even Her triumph and Her bracers can quell that pride. Perhaps it staggers—a little. Jarik is made of iron. Or god-metal, like his sword! The failures, the enslaving bracers, his inability to slay a greybeard with one arm after years of hate and dreams of vengeance ... these only make him hurt the more. They only make him more bitter. They only make him more determined! So much to prove, to be. Rats gnawing at his soul.

Jarik, Jarik ... poor Jarik. Duped servant of the Iron Lords. Bearer of a god-sword. Wearer of god-bonds. Enforced (duped?) servant of Milady Snowmist. Poor Jarik! None to love including self, and none to belong to or possess.

And Kirrensark thought, *What a waste!*

"We lived near the shore, among fisher-folk for some time. Two years ..." Jarik waved a hand carelessly; it did not matter how long, that gesture said. A hundred years ... "They welcomed us because I had healed one of them. Perhaps they thought me a wizard. But I healed no more. I could not. It's ... it's Oak who does that. He came on me no more, among them. They suffered us to remain because I worked, and Torsy worked—and *she* had some knowledge of healing herbs!"

An oarsman stumped up onto the stern-to-bow walkway. He shot a glance at the two in the prow, and turned to empty his pot into the sea. His wastes joined those of thousands, perhaps millions of others since first men learned to ply the green waters. The sea accepted stool and urine, swallowed them without noticing. The oarsman leaned on the rail. He was a young man, of Kirrensark-wark. He had been called Coon so often and for so long that some did not even know his proper name. His leggings were leather once tawny and now walnut-hued and splotched even darker. The tunic he wore over them, covering his arm to mid-forearm in loose sleeves and his legs to mid-thigh, had once been brown and now was faded to a hazelnut hue. His leathern belt, broad and thick and thrice studded with bosses of bronze like amber cabochons, was a hand's length longer than he was around. Its end was pulled through its brass ring, doubled back, looped over, and pulled through that loop. It dangled before him, copper-riveted at the tip. A little eating dagger no more than a foot long hung sheathed on his right hip and buskins shod his feet.

So were dressed the men aboard *Seadancer*. This one, Coon, wore a storm-hat of stiffened sealskin against the sun, for no storm was present or imminent. His hair sprang from beneath the ungainly hat, strawy as Jarik's and falling onto his shoulders, as Jarik's did.

He had lived in Kirrensark-wark all his life, Coon had; a span of seventeen years. In that time he had seen the god but twice, and then a third time only two weeks ago. The day after the advent of Jarik. *She* had come to see Jarik. *She* had taken Jarik up to Cloudpeak, her mountaintop keep. Next day he was back, wearing the shining bracers, from Her. And two days later the ship had been fitted and provisioned and launched, with Kirrensark commanding (or Jarik? Or Her?). Aboard were forty others, under the sail of yellow barred with red.

It was the greatest excitement of Coon's life. To do something, at last! To put to sea, on a fiercely staring hawkship! Gone ahawking! This was adventure!

Of a sudden and like a god Jarik had come upon the wark. To save Kirrensark and dine with him and attract the god at once, next day, and go off with Her. It was easy to hate such a man, and him so young, and unfriendly—so inward. Yet because of him, that wearer of the Black Sword, Coon had embarked on the greatest adventure of his life. It was hard to hate the provider of such an opportunity! But now... after ten days of dull sea-scudding, of piddling over the side and sitting on the pot that etched a ring in one's hocks, and emptying it over the side—to leeward, to leeward, else that which one no longer wanted would return, instanter! Now it was easier again to consider hating the wearer of the god-armlets, the wearer of the Black Sword of god-metal. The surly intimate of the wark's firstman. Adventure? Here was no adventure! Hissing along over the water. *Phup-phup-phup* over hedgerow waves and *slp-slp-sslp* of wake. No wood to chop or women to watch or animals to hear or even oars to pull. Following a *bird*...

Coon, from where he stood bored and starting to feel sorry for himself for he was seventeen and found adventure dull, and Jarik and Kirrensark at the prow near the rearing wooden head with its fierce yellow-painted eyes... all stared at the bird that led them.

The bird of Her. The gull of the Lady of the Snowmist. Their map, their beacon, their direction finder and sailing instructor and true ship's master; their leader. On it flew. Southward and westward, wings seldom flapping. It was a bird-servant of the god on the earth, of the Lady of the Snowmist. It soared, it streaked. It flashed in the sunlight. It made no sound and seldom flapped its wings.

Gods should keep to themselves, Coon thought. Their sorcerous doings and missions made men nervous, and weary of doing nothing.

Coon did not even know what they sought. Jarik knew.

On the Isle of Osyr was a temple and in the temple a statue of Osyr. It held a staff or wand. The Lady of the

Snowmist wanted that wand. Jarik was to fetch it to Her. That was his mission for Her. (While his mission for the Iron Lords was to slay Her!) He had sought to sword Her and that divine lady in white and silver and soft grey had eluded him, for she was a god. She struck him senseless. When he awoke she had bound him with the bracers she called the Bands of Snowmist. She had but two choices, she said: to slay him or to control him. Should he succeed and bring Her the White Rod of Osyr, she would remove the bracers. Jarik had told her the promise he had of the Iron Lords:

"Now you are an ally of the Iron Lords. Soon you will be the most favored of men in the world."

She heard, and she gave him her promise:

"You have *my* word that you will do as I bid now or suffer unendurable cold and pain and the horror in your mind of colliding worlds; and that once you have accomplished what I bid and returned to me with the White Rod of Osyr, you shall be free of the Bands of Snowmist. And those are *my* promises to you, Jarik of the Black Sword." And that was all.

He rebelled, and learned thus the agony of the Bands. He gained no other promise from her. Serve or suffer the unbearable. And Jarik knew that he was the least favored and most miserable man in the world. And she who owned him called him not yet a man.

Kirrensark's cousin Ahl coveted the wark's rule. Snowmist obtained promises from them both, and made assurances. Kirrensark's high seat would be safe while he fared to sea for Her. And so Jarik set forth, at the behest of Her he was to have slain. Jarik Blacksword who had been Orrikson Jarik and then Strodeson Jarik: agent of the Iron Lords and now unwilling agent of their sister Karahshisar, the Lady of the Snowmist. It was on this hated hawk-prowed ship of Lokusta he sailed. As shipmate he had the man on whom he had so long ago vowed vengeance: Kirrensark One-hand who had been Kirrensark Long-haft, the Hawker.

Allied with his enemies? Jarik was yet unsure which were enemies and which were not. The Iron Lords said that Snowmist was evil and she said that they were, that he was a mere tool. And Jarik wondered if it were a curse, that he had been found and adopted so long ago, rather than left to die as a result of abandonment by the parents whose names even the gods did not know.

The Iron Lords said that Snowmist had bidden his parents abandon him. She said that she had not. And Jarik ... *What is true? What is not true? Who lies to me? Or do they all? A hoe in a strong hand, she called me—a rusty hoe. A tool. No, No*!

"Men came," Coon heard Jarik mutter, and Coon jerked. He strained to hear over the hiss and slurp of the water that furled past *Seadancer*. Dully, talking to himself and the sea and the unhearing gods as much as to the bearded big man at his side, Jarik bespoke his memories.

"There were three of them, off a hawk-prowed ship. They slew Torsy. They raped and killed, and my mind fled me when I found their victims. I took the Black Sword from its altarstone in the village's center and I tracked those three men. After a day, I caught up to them." Jarik stared ahead, at the water, at the horizon, at nothing. "They are dead."

Three, Coon thought, and *three*, Kirrensark thought. He said, "You slew them all three?"

"Yes! I, alone!" Jarik's hand slapped the scabbard running down alongside his leg.

"All three," Kirrensark said, as from a clogged throat. Phlegm, perhaps. He said, "You were not wounded?"

"I was not. The Black Sword and I were one. My mind had fled. Only after that slaying did I seem to—to awake. I fight *morbrin*, Kirrensark. I know nothing when I fight. I don't think. I just fight and when it is over I see what I have done, and wonder at my prowess."

Kirrensark well remembered how Jarik, a stranger,

had come racing in to his aid—to his rescue! He slew one assailant with five blows, while the man got off only two with his ax—both turned on Jarik's shield. Kirrensark downed one. His murderous nephew fled them, and Kirrensark had to stay Jarik, who would have pursued and doubtless slain. The one Kirrensark had wounded asked for death, which Kirrensark would not grant. Jarik would. He did, with grim efficiency. And then the stranger who had slain two strangers to save a stranger became a pleasant youth, polite and respectful. Until next day, when he had deliberately sought to provoke Kirrensark to fight him, and the firstman had offered his life.

This youth who could be polite and respectful, Kirrensark knew, was very, very dangerous. Now he knew too what Jarik knew: that Jarik was not quite sane. And now he was silent again while *Seadancer* fled on south and west and Kirrensark, standing silent beside Jarik, well believed that he had slain three, one day less than three weeks ago.

Bored, Handeth the Hounder began ascending the mast, all unbidden, to see if he could espy the faintest hint of shore or tree or mountaintop. Careless in the ennui of boredom, Handeth slipped. He cursed, and began again to climb.

The ship followed the god-bird. Gane the Dogged and Seramshule haggled over the amber amulets they sought to trade, only for something to do. The god-bird, white and graceful in the sunlight, bore south and west. Coon—who had begun as "Coon-face" but had fought over that and accepted the shortened version—leaned on the side while he strained to hear Jarik's next words. Coon had seen no lord or king and had seen the god though never up close. Jarik, like him or not, was the most important man in the world. Just now.

"You have done death on eight, then," Kirrensark said. A few paces away Coon's narrowed eyes widened and then shut tight when seawater forced its brine-stinging way in. "Six, and those two who sought to deal me the shadow-death."

"Eight," Jarik said, "and seven." He spoke dully, not bragging, while staring ahead at nothing. Perhaps at the god-bird. Perhaps at the sky, which was the watery blue of an old man's eyes. "Ten off hawkships, for when I returned to the village of fishers, it was under attack. They were the shipmates of those I'd slain. The fishermen were defending, sort of. The Black Sword was their magical beacon that should have called the Iron Lords to protect them. I did not know that. I had it, that Sword. Men of the village died, because of me."

"But you—"

"I attacked the attackers. I was *morbrin*: the machine-that-fights. The wolf with a sword. By the time I had hewed through to their fore, I had slain several and wounded many. By the time they fled—for the fishermen rallied—I had slain seven. So the Iron Lords told me. I didn't know."

"The Iron Lords," Kirrensark said. He spoke quietly, prompting. He would not argue that Jarik had saved, whether he caused death or no; Kirrensark would not strive against another's desire to wallow in self-blame and pity.

Coon's adam's apple bobbed. Fifteen men! Fifteen corpses, like a wake behind the restlessly plowing ship that was Jarik Blacksword! And ... the Iron Lords. He had spoken with them, too! This man *knew* gods, and he was so young!

"They came," Jarik said. "Those gods all in black iron, masked in blue-black iron. Faceless—though I think it is not iron, but better: the god-metal. They slew the wounded hawkers. Fire came from their black swords. The attackers were burned. Fried. Consumed. They are gods!"

He went silent again, while he called up images of the past behind his eyes.

The ship ran on, light-footed, for the wind seemed to follow the gull. Sorcery. Full-sailed ship plunging easily behind a shining bird that rested only by night. Every helm and sword and ax was locked up in the little compartment astern, under the steering platform. Men retained their daggers for cutting rope or food or paring nails or cleaning beneath them. Only firstman Kirrensark kept his weapons, and Jarik, who was not subject to his orders.

Both wore daggers and Jarik's sword hung down his leg and Kirrensark had his evil ax. It was not wise for a one-handed man to continue to use the ax, but Kirrensark had more pride than smarts. With Jarik, he had neither. Though he did not wear it now, Jarik had very fine armor, quintuply linked dark chain that glinted blue in the sun. The mailcoat resembled the skin of a black snake sunning itself. Sinuous. Fluid and scintillant. Decorative bronze links flashed red-gold at the hems of sleeve and skirt.

The leader, huge of frame and accustomed to firstman's authority long held and wise with years, had caused the materials of war to be locked away astern. Ten days crammed together were long and long, and last night Runner had almost found a new sheath for his dagger, in Tole's breast. Others had restrained them, secretly glad for the excitement and striving. Jarik had looked ferocious. Kirrensark had railed at them in the manner of a firstman and ship's master; then he sympathized and quietly reasoned like a father, and they slept, all of them. Keeping their daggers.

Today Tole sat at the steerboard stern position, while Runner sat up forward to larboard, under Kirrensark's nose.

"Do you know the names of the Lords of Iron, Kirrensark?" Jarik asked, saying *Kiddensahk* in their language of unpronounced r's; he was *Jaddik* and very nearly *Yaddik*. He squinted at the wave-reflected sunlight.

Coon jerked at his voice. Coon had been thinking of

flashing weapons, and fifteen men dead in blood—and of what lay behind the maidenly apron of Tinye, back home. He heard Kirrensark's reply: "Death! And Death again, and Trickery! Those are their names, the Iron Lords!"

Almost, Jarik smiled. "Worse," he said, without ever glancing at the master of the ship he rode. "Destruction, and Annihilation, and Dread. Those are the names of the faceless Lords of Iron in their masks of iron. Dread is the oldest and he says little, very little. There is much Dread, in silence."

"Aye," Kirrensark said, thinking how much better he knew Jarik, in these few minutes of talking after ten days of near silence. Now Jarik had talked of Jarik. He was at once less dreadful, and more.

Fifteen men. And him...what? Twenty, perhaps? Nineteen? A little older? Kirrensark did not know. Nor would anyone ever be certain again of Jarik's age, for he would never say how long he had dwelt in Blackiron, that village of fishermen across the (impassable!) mountains. Or could not, perhaps. He was surely older than eighteen, and younger than twenty-and-five.

Wasn't he? Weren't there forty years of bitterness and hurt and hate in his face, of frustration and Outsiderness in his pale eyes? No; it but seemed so. No lines marked his face. He still had his youth, light on the vine despite a heaviness of soul.

Fifteen men! Fifteen corpses.

Fifteen war-men sent into the dark, to the abode of the Dark Brother. Mateless and lonely while he nursed his hatred of yellow-haired Shralla of the Sun and Seramis her parted mate, the Dark Brother ever sought new companions in the dark, more companions. Fifteen had Jarik sent him this year, with edge of sword. All recently, and at least ten of them from the ships he hated. The long, stripe-sailed ships with the heads of preying birds mounted atop their high-rearing prows.

Now Jarik rode such a ship.

He was tricked, humiliated, defeated, embondaged, bidden, *sent*.

And yet his pride remained. It soared high as the flashing gull of the god on the earth; she who was served by the gull and by this hawk-ship, and by Jarik. He stared ahead, an abysmal umbrage on his mind.

Then he whirled from the prow.

Kirrensark fell back from the twisting of Jarik's features, which were not unhandsome though carved as if by a hand-ax and frozen in bitterness. His thick-backed hand wrapped around the red leather wound about his sword's hilt to disguise that black handle and mitigate its oil-smooth slipperiness. From his sheath without a sound swept the Black Sword that was more dull than refulgent, and the more deadly looking for being so. He shouted.

"Turn, turn, turn! Cease following that fell bird! Surely we are beyond *her* sway, now! Turn! I abjure your god, and *her* service unto pox and plague!"

He stood a heroic figure, sword on high and hair snapping about his face from the ceaseless wind that drove them. A superb figure, tall and rangy and muscled with liquid steel in every inch of his body. And he shouted defiance at the thrice-distant Lady of the Snowmist.

No matter the distance. She replied.

Cold rose in his wrists. Terrible cold. Emanating from the Bands of Snowmist, it seized them as though it were winter and he had plunged his hands through ice into a mountain pool. Cold attacked. It slashed at his arms and into them and spread into his body as a physical force. Abruptly his teeth were chattering, though he stood under the bright sun. From the seamless bracers of silvery god-metal and god-magic, his arms were as if frozen. The Black Sword dropped. It did not clang, but struck decking and imbedded its point. A weapon of incredible sharpness and un-notched edge. A god-weapon though it spat no fire as did the identical ones carried by the Iron Lords.

Orrikson Jarik gasped, whitened, felt his fingers numbing. Strodeson Jarik grunted, groaned, shivered. Jarik Blacksword tried to bite off his voice but cried out anyhow. Every face aboard *Seadancer* turned toward him. Eyes widened and stared. The nerve-assaulting impossibility of burning cold slashed into his chest.

"SLAVE!" he shouted in a voice of agony. "I am her slave, the foul bitch-god of Kirrens-ah!"

He was overwhelmed by pain and cold he could not bear and live, and he fell down. He lay white and in agony from her bands of seamless, silver-gleaming god-metal.

2

The Saga of Oak, the Healer

"Jarik Blacksword, is it? Two men in one, a confused troubled troublous treacherous brain, result of a child and boy crushed again and again with more than he could bear. The Man who is Two Men! Man? Not yet!"
—The Lady of the Snowmist

"It is impossible that contrary attributes should belong at the same time to the same subject."
—Aristotle

Jarik awoke, kneeling beside his father's corpse. Smoke billowed and Jarik's eyes streamed. The hawk-men were gone. His knees ached and his nostrils stung. He was eight years old and his hands were all bloody. The odors of smoke and blood and death blanketed his nostrils and Torsy was screaming his name. He told her that he was there, right there, and bade her stop screaming.

Torsy broke off. She stared at him as though he were strange. Her eyes were all red from weeping. It was she who was strange, he saw, all huge-eyed and brooding. Instinctively or preternaturally, he knew that Torsy would never never be the same again, or quite normal. But then neither would he, naturally.

He looked around, without wondering at how he had come here from the woods, and why his knees were sore as if he had long held this position. Bewildered, he looked about him. The world was misted with smoke and carpeted with corpses and coagulated blood. It was brown and gleamed metallically. Tomash-ten, Oceanside, had been destroyed; annihilated; extirpated. (*And Dread, don't forget Dread*, the thought came into his mind, but he did not know why. Then.) His mind staggered under a load it could not bear and remain wholly sane, ever. And he knelt over his supine father—who had been *bandaged*!

Days later, when they were asea in the little boat that had been Othik's, Torsy told him it was he who had bandaged his father, though he was dead already. And when she had spoken to him he had told her that his name was not Jarik.

He had told her his name was Oak.

Jarik's staggered, unbearably assaulted brain had found a way to let Oak be born, and live, and Oak was *good*.

Nor did Oak like Jarik.

I fell down that day, Jarik thought, *unconscious. And I dreamed or saw visions—I even saw the Lady of the Snowmist, years and years before I ever even heard of her, much less saw her! And I—*

But now he had hurtled forward in time, and was nearly twice as old. One night in a dream (?) the Guide had come and shown him the vision that he somehow knew was the collision and destruction of two worlds. Worlds like this one. (That was silly, though, because they were round, and how could the world be round?) And Jarik remembered that his Guide had said, *Thus did I depart*.

You are a God on the Earth, Jarik said.

I am a god on the earth, (something)*son Jarik*.

B-but—what have I seen?

It is your birthright and your conception you have seen, Jarik. You saw two that were one, and when they became one they shattered and were nothing. You are a twoness that must be a oneness, and that can come about only by your taking on a third part, which will unify you into one.

I—I do not understand! the sleeping Jarik had said then, or rather thought to the Guide, and he echoed it now: *I still do not understand! Why has my Guide never come back to me? What did he mean; what did the vision mean?*

I do not understand!

Nor will you, nor can you. It will be agony to you that you do not understand, and are two both at once, (something)son Jarik, and for that I am sorry. Yet the agony will continue when you are whole—three as one, although it will be a different sort of agony and you will know happiness.

(Happiness? What is happiness?)

Some happiness, the Guide went on, as if He had not heard. *A part of you is a tree, and a part of you lies on an island, and you—you lie on the ship of Kirrensark, Jarish. You and I will meet again.*

Then the Guide was gone, and Jarik awoke in his home in Ishparshule-wark, and it was not the Guide's staff he clutched, but his own. That night he had at last, late, come to puberty and nascent manhood.

Did I experience only a dream? Did it just return, or am I remembering? Am I conscious or not? Was it a vision, prescient or post-, or some god-sent miracle that could be called alternate reality or . . . just a dream?

New trauma had added new tangles to the threads of the unfinished fabric of his life, and the weavers wove, who sewed the fabric of human lives.

Now it all changed again, and he had slain Stath and been exiled from Isparshule-wark, forever, and he was coming along the beach when he saw that two men had Torsy and one was using her. He had been pondering that he seemed to have left his body and *flown*, spotting a village not far from them. Now he forgot that. The two men looked up to see themselves being charged by a youthful madman.

They rose up with their weapons to meet him, sword and ax and shields, and in minutes they were dead in their blood on the strand. Jarik seemed to waken from the *morbrin* trance that had come upon him, making him a kill-machine, and he looked at Torsy. She lay on her side. Her huge eyes stared. Jarik saw with horror that blood smeared her loins and was coming from her left nostril, and from the corner of her mouth.

His sword slipped forgotten from his fingers. He shook off his shield as *he started for her. She was hurt and bleeding. He must help her. "Jarish," she said weakly, and poor Torsy was sobbing. They had hurt her and made her bleed and cry. He went to her and squatted. He pressed her back. "Be still," he said, almost harsh in his single-mindedness. His hands ran over her and checked her blooded loins. She was not injured. The blood had already stopped flowing. It had come from the last tissue of her maidenhead. He touched her nose with fingers light as down. It was not broken. Her lip was cut, and bled. Blood from nose and lip mingled. "Be still, very still," he said, and carefully, gently, he tugged out her lip and turned it. "Gaaah," Torsy said in her throat, staring up at him while he discovered that the tooth to the left of the two front biters was chipped.* They hit her in the face, *he* thought, rather coolly, and the broken tooth cut her lip. *It was cut, and bruised. He saw that it would swell and stay swollen for some time. But there was no permanent damage, nothing to disfigure Torsy's face, and he knew that the mouth healed itself better than any other part of the body. With her head back, the bleeding of her nose was ending. The tooth should be filed, to get the sharp edges off. He had no file. Later, then. With her head between both hands, he closed his eyes. He pressed in only a little,* seeing. *She snuffed, swallowing blood. Her head was all right; he* saw *no other injury. Eyes closed, he passed his hands down her body, as though lightly stroking. She quivered. Her eyes fixed a wide gaze on him. He* saw *no wound. She was hale. He would not use the herbs; both her mouth and loins were well equipped to take care of themselves. Ah— the one called hart's tail, he* saw, *might be useful on her lip, for he* saw *that it reduced swelling.*

"Jarish—"

"*Call me not Jarik! I am Oak, the Healer!*"

She trembled, blinking, and kept her gaze fixed on him while his hands traced down her willowy body, all the way to her feet.

"You—you saved me! You killed them both!"

He was horrified. "*No! He* killed them, *the bloody vicious barbarian—Jarik! His heart pounded and his blood ran high and hot the while, for* Jarik *loved it! I* Jarik *killed them! And he enjoyed it! I had nothing to do with it. I am no killer. I have nothing to do with killing. I heal; I am the healer, Oak.*"

Oak! Oak the Healer! Oak, in Jarik's body, hating Jarik. For Jarik was the Man who was Two . . . and both of them hated Jarik.

It happened again, later the same day. Torsy and Jarik left the strand. They struggled through the dense wood, toward the fishing village he knew was there. They came upon a man. A trapper who had fallen afoul of his own trap and was unconscious and bloody. Torsy squatted beside him. She slipped, and slapped down a hand to catch herself, and when that hand came up all blood Jarik stared, and knew horror, and

"*Let me see that hand,*" Oak said. "*Quickly.*"

"Jarish, it's not even—"

"*Don't call me that!*" Oak said, *with vehemence unto viciousness.* "*He* kills. *I* heal. *Ah. Silly little girl . . . this isn't hurt at all. You just slipped in his blood and got it on you. Here, get out of the way and let me see this man. Ummm. See that plant there—there, with the funny leaves. Yes, that one—of course. Pull it up. Don't break it off; pull it up, and find more. Bring me them. Go along, girl. Go! Now . . . um hmm,*" Oak said, *lifting the man's eyelid, letting it slip back over the blue eye.* "*The shock . . . he's unconscious. Blood-flow is slowed but it won't stop, with that clean-through wound. We must stop it."*

Soon an arrangement of knotted cords and a stick slowed the flow of blood from the trapper's leg, transpierced by his own trip-spear. Angrily muttering, more surely than not, Oak took the roots Torsy brought him and wasted water: he washed the dirt-dribbling roots, and his hands, and the roots. After that he made a thorough mess of roots and hands by rolling the tuberish things between his palms.

"Should be more like paste," Oak muttered, applying the ruined roots to the man's wound. The cord he had wrapped around the leg and twisted tight, using the stick he had cut with Jarik's knife, had slowed the blood's flow to a scarlet ooze. The semi-crushed roots soon make it thicken, and stop.

"You . . . you fixed him!" Torsy enthused.

"Hardly," he told her. *"Remember that plant. It thickens liquids. Such as blood."*

"What—what's it called?"

"I don't know. Spare me your silly questions. The cord around his leg stops the blood. Won't let it flow to the wound at all. The root is a thickener. We will have to loosen the cord every now and then. Remember that."

"Why—?"

He stared at her. No, he glowered, this surly, businesslike, Jarik-hating healer called Oak who shared Jarik's body. It's important. I have said it. Blood has to flow through the body. Otherwise the skin dies. He rots. He should stay here a while. A long while, in truth, but he'd best be got to his own wark.

He told her they must construct a litter, and Torsy thought that he was very wise, this unfriendly healer who shared the body of her foster-brother and hated him the while. Very, very wise. He knew more about the body, and healing, than anyone. Tentatively, her head on one side, she said, "Oak?"

Oak the scry-Healer glowered at her.

Thus they saved a man of the fishers' wark called Blackiron, at the foot of the mountain keep of the Iron Lords, and thus were Jarik and Torsy accepted into the village. But Oak did not return. Nor did Jarik know what Oak knew. Torsy remembered all that Oak had done, and said, and she gained respect among them as a healer. Jarik had little. They were fishers, at peace, and had little need of a strong young weaponer who knew nothing of fishing. He learned.

They abode there. And time passed, and then Torsy and Alye and Nevre went one spring day into the woods to gather nuts before the squirrels and wild pigs did. Jarik was to meet Alye, and when he found her not at the assigned place he did not long wait. Patience was a quality he did not possess. He went looking. Found their trail. Found Torsy and Nevre. They had been used, and beaten, and cut, and chopped with iron blades. Blood was everywhere and they were dead.

The people of Blackiron backed from the bleak and horrifying creature that strode through the little village, and took the Black Sword from the Blackiron Stone in Blackiron; that unrusted and rustless blade that was taboo. Still a silent awful stalker, he seized the sword and rushed it through the air, black and sharp and shining after a century, and he strode back into the wood and vanished.

When he overtook Torsy's killers, over a day later, the trio of men from hawk-head ships was as half a man against the maniacal animal who came ravening upon them with his awful black sword. They died. Alive, shrinking, Alye was there, and alive. Jarik bladed his sword in the blood-splashed sod and went to her. Horror was a dark clawing force in his brain as he started to bend over her. It rose up like ground-mist, and whelmed his mind.

Bruised, bloodied, much ill-used, Alye appeared to be in shock. Oak, tracing his fingers over her while she

*cringed all ashudder, learned more; he saw within her.
She was internally torn and ruined of body and mind; he
saw that she was hopelessly insane. Oak the Healer could
do nothing. He rose, with tears rilling down his face that
was Jarik's face save more stern, and he retreated from the
brain and body he presently commanded. This time, he let
Jarik know with certainty what he knew. Then Oak was
gone, and the body fell to the ground.*

Jarik awoke, and he *knew*. He gazed on the torn turf.
The splashes of blood and the corpses. He knew that he
had slain three men and that none of the blood on him was
his own. And he looked upon Alye. The tears Oak had left
to dry on his face were joined by new ones. He blinked
hard while he turned and drew the Black Sword from the
ground. Then he turned back to Alye and did what he
must; he ended a helpless animal's permanent misery.

Another scar was left in his mind, and the Weavers
wove, and he returned to Blackiron to find the attack in
progress. He ended it. One he much liked was wounded,
and it was Jarik who groaned, reeled, dropped the Sword
that had sent the hawkers flying, clutched his head . . . *and
it was Oak who bent over the injured youth. He began
examining the wound, though seemingly superficially;
Oak the Healer had no need of probes.* The Iron Lords
were there. They saw.

Oak called for Torsy to bring the remedy kit. A voice
that sounded as if it came up from the depths of an
iron-walled well asked if he were Oak the Healer. Oak
confirmed. "And are you he who took up the black sword
and slew these attackers?"

Oak looked up and his reply was a shout, even to those
who were Gods on the Earth: "NO!" And he returned to
his business, which was scrying hurts and healing them.

Later they asked again, when Oak had done.

"I am not Oak the Healer," he told the Iron Lords. "My
name is Jarik."

"Ah," one Lord of Iron said as if in an aside, from
within his mask of blued black iron, "once there are no

wounded to tend, he reverts to the main personality, then." The helm-masks of his brother-gods nodded. Only they, however, understood what had been said.

"Oak," Jarik murmured, flailing his head as he lay on the decking of Kirrensark's ship. "O-oak . . . heal us! Heal me!" Asea without a helsman, Jarik and *Seadancer* alike.

"Jarik—" That from Kirrensark, who stayed Coon from squeezing more sea-water over Jarik's forehead. The bracers were the temperature they should have been, metal that was warmer where the sun touched it and cold nowhere on this spring day in southerly waters.

As he regained consciousness, knowing a little more about himself and yet a little less because still there were no explanations, Jarik heard a voice call from above, up the mast: "LAND! I see land!"

3

The Isle of Osyr

The fate of man lies with the gods;
His life's fabric is by their leave.
Let no human misdoubt the odds!
The gods decide; the weavers weave.

The infant pules, and mayhap grows old—
Its life's fabric is by gods' leave.
Changes come, mind and body enfold
The fabric that the weavers weave.

Each hap marks the mind with a scar,
All lead to what he will achieve.
Mayhap each aids; doubtless some mar.
Events befall, while weavers weave.

The ship was a gigantic insect moving in toward shore on
many legs. The sail was rolled. Men had taken down the
mast and stretched it the length of the ship, and lashed it
fast. The many moving legs of *Seadancer* were of wood,
wielded by grunting rowers clad in mail. They sweated.
Seabirds wheeled and soared about that strange insect,
keening, scolding.

"We'll not suffer from want of food," Seramshule said, while he strung his bow. He was gazing ashore, and he was not frowning.

Skimpy of freeboard and easily handled, *Seadancer* had ruddered half around this tree-grown land with its bluish inland mountains. The close-in maneuvering had shown them no inhabitants, and men wondered. They were about halfway around, they felt, when men shouted at sight of this hospitable strand.

Now they rowed in. The water foamed white over the oars and the strand sparkled. The dark wall of treeline began to display individual trunks. Now the trees seemed taller. Spaces began to appear in what had been a mass of greenery. Even so, those spaces were few. Every man rowed, save Kirrensark, and Tole who was at the steering oar. Jarik rowed. Weapons were out and had been buckled on or laid to hand. Swords, axes, spears; a few bows and quivers of arrows.

This was Kerosyr—Ker Osyr; Isle of Osyr—for here the gull had led them.

Unless it stretched many miles south or west, the isle was no enormous one. A jumbled collection of woods with the look of virginity and low mounts far out off the western coast of Akkharia, where Jarik had known his first eight winters. Shallow of draft, *Seadancer* cruised through water less and less deep, easily approaching the beach. Bits of glassy sand sparkled. Roots of spruce bound the ship's tarred oaken planking below the waterline, so that she was sinuous as a smallish whale.

"Up oars!"

And *Seadancer* swept forward under the morning sun, oars high, and was beached.

First they must find fresh water, and fill their vessels to be stored on the ship. Men might have to take precipitate leave of an unknown land. If that was accompanied by pursuit that prevented their putting in elsewhere within a short time, drinkable water aboard was far more important than food or the speedy undertaking of a mission, upon making land.

The weapons were unnecessary. Kirrensark heard a bit of grumbling, that he had made them stand offshore and sleep aboard ship last night. They could have slept ashore. Here was nothing to fear! Finding and collecting fresh water was swiftly accomplished, without adventure.

"The owl and the wolf prefer the dark," Kirrensark reminded grumblers.

"Hawks do not fear owls," Hounder muttered low.

Though we come off a hawk-ship, Jarik thought, *surely we are the wolves.*

"Enough talk of yesterday and the night-that-was," Kirrensark said, leading them up the strand. "We are to—what's become of our gull?"

Perhaps it was about and perhaps not; there were many gulls, aye, and terns, and in the woods a raven called raucously. No man knew which of these noisy squealy birds was *their* gull, their guide. The Lokustans looked at each other. Weathered hands gripped straps of shield and hafts, of spear.

Armed, helmeted, bearing hide-covered bucklers, wearing brass-studded leathern coats or jerkins, they gathered on the strand at wood's edge. Day lay on them with its full light, and accoutrements flashed. Three men wore leather coats closely sewn with iron links, and another a similar coat of bronze links that had been his father's, and Delath Berserker wore his supple leathern jerkin that flashed with line after line of overlapping scales of brass, terribly bright in the sunlight. He wore brass bracers, too. Once maiden-raiders had come from another wark, and the first girl they saw was Delath's daughter Climinsekye, who was twelve. She was first to see the five raiders. Delath her father was second. She screamed. Delath set off running, bellowing like a maddened bull. By the time others reached them, three of the raiders from the other wark lay dead or nearly and of the two who fled, one left behind his sword and three fingers.

Jarik wore his mailcoat of unusually, nigh unbelievably good chain. Better than any had been or deemed could be made. It was of the Iron Lords, though of iron, not their metal. Links of bronze decorated it to flash amid the field of blued iron. His bronze-buckled belt was broad, and supported a short dagger and a long, and the scabbarded Black Sword whose tip hung at his ankle. Helmets were plain round pots, most lined with sponge and some with sponge and leather both. Jarik's helm was more pointed than any. With them they bore much length of sealskin rope.

A dove appeared from among the oak and holly and yew and rowan. White as a summer cloud, it flew to Jarik. It circled him. It lit on his mailed shoulder. Every man stared. Then the dove fluttered up, making Jarik squint and avert his face. It flew into the trees. A moment later it was back, to circle Jarik, and fly again into the trees.

"Another guide," Delath Berserker said, tight lipped.

"*She* is still with us," Kirrensark said.

Jarik showed no delight. Following their guide, they forged inland amid gooseberry and haw, hart's tongue and shrubs they could not name. Trees lofted tall all about them and Shralla's light was dimmed by them so that it crept down to the forest floor in diffident fingers. Here the growing season would be longer than five months stretched from four. Here winters would not be so hard, on Osyr's island. Here were more birds, and surely more game.

And more insects. This was not their land. They complained of the insects, and of the clamor of birds both familiar and strange. The dove led them inland amid the odor of spruce and minkweed and red-thorn bushes. Armored men under iron helms lined from the sea with sponge that never lost its own pellagic odor while taking on the smell of sweat. Bobbing shields of linden-wood, covered with hide mostly white—Jarik's was red, and bore a sword's black silhouette that seemed to slice through the boss. Long spears ending in wicked leaves of iron caused their bearers trouble amid branches and brush. Axes and a few swords also armed men who moved among the trees as they had scudded over the sea, behind a bird sent by Her.

"You did not shift to sword when you lost the arm," Jarik said, stating the obvious rather than ask the question.

"Pride," Kirrensark said. "I'd always carried an ax." And that was all.

"The sword would be better for you, now."

"I am not crippled."

"Less so with sword than with an ax. 'Ware this bush!"

"You will not provoke me, Jarik Blacksword. I will not be provoked by you." And Kirrensark added, from within his beard of grey and dark blond, "I have not had to fight for over a decade."

Jarik refused to let go. "You increase your danger by keeping to the ax. Tomorrow may always bring fighting, for so the weavers weave. The fifth step from now may bring fighting!"

This time the firstman made no reply. After many paces Jarik, scenting wild garlic without smiling, asked, "Why have you undertaken this mission for Her?"

"She is a god on the earth; she is our god. We serve Her. We do her bidding. While I am gone, and these loyal men with me, she will protect the wark from enemies— including my plotsome cousin Ahl."

They fared on. A man cursed the hawthorn he swore tried to take his spear from him. A man released the whippy branch of a bush, and it struck across the chin of the man behind him, who cursed and received apology even while others derided his complaint at so minor a blow. The trees lessened in their number. And lessened, for they were skirting a rocky rise like the bone of the land.

"The Lady of the Snowmist has always been there, Jarik Blacksword. She has never changed. Aye, now and again she comes to the wark and takes a young man up to her keep atop Cloudpeak . . . within Cloudpeak. Some say her voice changed, years and years ago, but it has remained the same since. She returns the man she takes in a day or so. His is happy, though he remembers nothing. Nor does he ever fall ill, throughout his life!"

All this Jarik knew. Ishparshule-wark over the mountain was within the province of Lady Snowmist, and Jarik had hoped to be Chosen. No. She had come while he was away from the wark, and she had Chosen Brathis. Brathis the God-Favored had been very, very popular thereafter—remembering nothing of his sojourn with Her—and Jarik had been all the more morose.

"She is the god," Kirrensark resumed, or went on. "She does not interfere in our affairs. When now and again she makes a request, we her protected people spring happily to carry it out."

Kirrensark, paying too much mind to his words, stumbled amid grey gorse. Jarik watched him catch himself with facility, using the rim of the shield strapped to his stump.

"And you, Jarik Blacksword. Remember you aught of your visit with her?"

"Aye. I remember everything," Jarik said.

So he thought. He thought he had all his memories. In truth he did not know how long he had lain unconscious while *Elye Isparela*, the Lady of the Snowmist, made his mind share with Her all the knowledge and memories it held. Nor had he knowledge of what else she'd done while he lay senseless and dreaming; what else she had taken from him.

"So. You serve the god. You do her bidding without question. Even to coming on this journey, solely to bear me on her business."

"Aye, Jarik Blacksword, though her requests are infrequently made. She told me this one is important to the wark."

"Taking me to the temple of Osyr on Ker Osyr?"

"Aye—but no. We are but to convey you to the isle, Jarik Blacksword. We cannot enter the temple. You will go in alone."

"Cannot enter? You mean will not?"

"Cannot. Whatever your business in the temple—she did not tell us—we are not to know, or to accompany you inside. We will wait, and return you to Her."

"Never has Jarik been so important as to have ship and armed men at his escort and disposal!" Jarik said, but without elation.

"You have pleased Her, Jarik."

"Not likely! The Iron Lords gave me this mailcoat, and left the Black Sword with me, and transported me across the impassable mountain . . . all so that I could kill her. I tried."

From the two nearest men, who heard, came gasps and stares. Jarik affected not to notice. He tried to look both cool and fierce. That made him resemble only a young man trying to look older, and evil. Yet doubly blond Delath *morbriner*, who was of about Kirrensark's age, stared without smiling. Perhaps he wondered how Jarik fought. None of them had seen that save Kirrensark and none at all had seen Oak, or knew of him.

"Nonetheless she chose you for the task, and us only as guides," Kirrensark said. "You did save my life."

Jarik's bitterness rose strong. "It was a fair trade. You ruined mine."

Kirrensark squeezed his eyes shut for a moment, and said nothing. He walked. They were approaching a long, long gentle slope, purpled here and there by foxglove.

"Your namesake," a man said, pointing upward.

The man nearest him looked, and nodded. His name was Climinseck: sparrowhawk. He plodded, legs and feet gone hot in leather leggings and buskins cross-wrapped with leathern straps.

"Perhaps I am sent because I displeased Her," Jarik opined aloud. "What if I do not emerge from the temple?"

"We will wait until Milady Snowmist summons us."

Kirrensark jerked his hand toward Jarik's silverbound wrist. "She is linked to you by the bracers. She will know if you are . . . slain."

"She'd not have sent us so far merely for one to be slain in an old temple," Handeth said, all in a grunt.

True, Jarik thought. *I hope! I wonder how I go about making my peace with this one-armed old greybeard who accepts my jibes with bravery beyond bravery—or is it the weakness of his years and debility?*

But would there be honor in that? Is it as hard to be other men as it is to be Jarik?

Jarik asked, "Can you tell me why you obey Her, Kiddensahk?"

"It is my pleasure. It is my duty. She is the god." The shrug of insouciant acceptance was implicit in Kirrensark's matter-of-fact words.

"So are the Iron Lords," Jarik said. "She is not *my* god! You know that I am forced to do her bidding, else I'd not be here. Do you know these Bands of hers give me the most awful sorceries, illusions, with the pain?"

"Yes."

With the sudden testiness of suspicion Jarik asked, "How can you know that?"

"When you rebelled, on the ship, both times. You did not lie still, Jarik Blacksword. We knew your suffering was of the mind."

"Did you touch the bracers?"

"Yes. They were not cold."

"At once?"

"No one touched them at once. That second time, on yesterday, I touched them soon after you fell. They were not cold, Jarik Blacksword."

"Sorcery. God-sorcery. They grow *freezing*, in two blinks of the eye! She did tell me that they would serve me, too; they will warn me of danger."

"We need no such on this hillside," Handeth said. "I can see farther than I can piss!"

Delath slipped and went to one knee. "Blighted

hillside!" Then, rising, "You have trouble seeing, Handeth?"

"Look over there. Nothing. Pasture-land running right into that mountain, so far it's blue. Must be two days' walk."

"Even in curses," Kirrensark said to Jarik, "there are blessings."

"What?"

"The worst storm waters the soil for the crops and fills the well."

"You talk like an old man, firstman of Kirrensark-wark!"

"I am an old man. I am twice your age, young Jarik Blacksword. I could be your . . . this walking reminds me of my years, and particularly this climbing!"

"You have not called a rest."

"I see no temple atop this blighted hill," Delath said.

"The dove of Her does not seem minded to rest," Kirrensark said.

"Her! Blight Her!"

"Gods blight," Kirrensark said evenly, "and men abide."

"You shock us, Jair-yik Karstarl," Delath said, though in no voice of shock. Others were shocked, that he mildly mocked the servant of the god, who the firstman had assured them was a mighty *akatir*—warrior; man of weapons—indeed.

Yes, Jarik mused. *Gods blight! And some gods lie. And Kirrensark abides. He slew, and he abides. My entire life was overturned by his slaying and I cannot abide. I have the nerves of a beaten pup, of a marten in wolf country. But he, blight him, he abides, serene as a cow with her cud!*

He said, "Know you aught of these unnatural bracers that bind me to Her and the quest she's put me on?"

"No. We know nothing of them, Jarik Blacksword. Save that they mark you as hers; she wears identical bracers on her slim wrists."

"Her armored wrists. I have seen them without armor,

Kirrensark. But not uncovered. The god...your god. Have you seen her face?"

"No."

"Have you seen her face, Jarik Blacksword?" Handeth asked.

"No. Nor the faces of the Iron Lords. All wear masks attacked to their helmets."

"I reckon all gods wear such helmasks," Handeth the Hounder said. "But you might have seen her face, Blacksword, and forgot!"

"Call me Jarik. I remember everything of my visit with her, Handeth," Jarik said, and he thought that he did. "Do we run onto trouble, Kirrensark, I'd feel better if the firstman among my *guides* wielded a sword, not the ax of a two-handed man."

"You have seen that I can use it," Kirrensark said blandly.

"We of Kirrensark-wark are not happy to hear you badsaying both our god and our firstman, Jarik Blacksword," Delath *morbriner* said. "Why do you continue to try to provoke a man who is too strong in the will not to fight you?"

"Why do you imitate the jaybird and flap your tongue, Delath?" Jarik asked.

Delath stopped and stared; Jarik stopped and returned the look. Every other man came to pause there on the hillside, and looked from Jarik to Delath to Kirrensark. Tole moved first. He walked, limping because he crossed the incline they climbed, toward Kirrensark. Two others made the groaning noises of disapproval. They too were stared at by men who would welcome activity and excitement, even the clashing of two of their number. None but doubted that the madness of *morbrin* would come on Delath, and he would destroy stormcloud Jarik. A few frowned, better at the business of thinking; would that not displease Her?

Wearing the face of a dead man, Kirrensark beat his palm on his thigh.

"I applaud mighty warriors," he said, and his voice too

was emotionless. He mocked them, and both knew it. Jarik's lips were very tight and he stared from beneath lowered brows. Delath's beard was white because he was so blond, not because of his age.

"We've but a little way to go," Kirrensark said, nodding upward. "Let us have no fighting. You are not boys, and I am not so helpless as to need a protector, Delath."

"He is—" Delath began, but broke off, and after that all knew there would be no fight.

They climbed the long, long slope all dotted with foxglove and burr-bush and stones in sunlight. The dove hovered above its summit, and alit. They climbed. They had seen no one. Heard no human sound, seen no human sign. Men cursed insects. Men stumbled. Stones rolled away down the slope and once Tole picked one up and threw it, with all his strength. Then he took up his spear again, and again he ascended among the others. Men cursed stones. They saw a peregrine, and envied it its soaring freedom. Men sweated in leather and wool and armor they did not need, and the bird awaited them.

They reached the summit, and looked beyond, and were shocked.

4

The Temple of Osyr

Let no human misdoubt the odds!
The gods decide; the weavers weave.

The hill was a freak. They had ascended a very long and
gentle slope, with considerable vegetation. Now they
stood on the very brow of a sheer cliff that fell and fell,
and was naught but stone, in grey and tan. The Lokustans
looked down into a valley that was not huge. Yet it could
have contained the dwelling area, if not the grazing and
growing lands, of their own Kirrensark-wark. It was only
partially grassed, so that they could see yellowish and pale
russet soil, dotted with clumps of pale green and with
boulders and stones ranging up to the size of sheds and
bigger. And they saw the temple.

It was old, old. An old temple to an old god men
assumed dead. It had been repaired—not well—and
added to, over the years. Patchwork. Even from here it
could be seen that all the pillars of the portico did not
match. Nor was it symmetrical, that structure of mingled
wood and grey, mica-glinting stone. They knew north,
from where they stood, even without looking at the sun,
for those splashes of orangey-green up one wall of the
temple were moss.

Two-and-twenty men of Lokusta stood, armed and

armored, and looked down upon the temple of Osyr.

They saw no animal in the treeless valley. They saw no sign that humanity had existed here for many, many years. They watched the white dove of Her fly down to the temple, and circle it, and flap back to them. In silence they gazed, to watch the dove flap over them and down the incline. It vanished among the trees they had quitted.

It had brought them here, and it had shown them their goal. Now it departed and they were left to their own abilities.

At last Kirrensark said, "Here we wait. There lies the temple. We can go no farther. The quest is yours, Jarik Blacksword."

They waited, watching, for many minutes. In the valley, nothing moved. Two men busied themselves making loops in the ends of long thick ropes. They knotted and re-knotted them. From the woods behind and below, a cuckoo called. Jarik received stares and exaggerated politeness while he tested the knots. The ropes were long enough, he was assured. Handeth was good at judging distances, and lengths. A few feet above the loop in one rope had been built up a big bulging knot. The other loop was a slip-noose.

"I will tug when I am ready to come up," Jarik said. "I will tighten the noose around the Rod of Osyr. I'll step into the other loop."

"You will be pulled up, Jarik Blacksword," Handeth said, as if reassurance were necessary. Kirrensark nodded. Others nodded.

Jarik fastened his helmet-strap and removed his weapons-belt. Rearranging it as a baldric, he slung the Black Sword on his back. The hilt, in its wrapping in red leather that old women had chewed and chewed, poked up above his left shoulder. He slung his scarlet-faced shield behind, too, so that it covered him from above the waist to the backs of his knees. He would not take his spear.

"A warrior carries a spear," Runner told him.

Jarik remembered something Steed Blackwelder of the fishers' village of Blackiron had done with his face, and Jarik imitated it: he winked.

Oddly, it was Delath who laughed.

Two men eased the rope loops over the precipice and stepped back, stretching the heavier line to them; the second took it around his waist. Jarik was no small man, or short. Shield, weapons, helm and chaincoat added another seventy-five pounds to his weight. At the edge of the cliff, he lay down on his belly on the rope. Facing the others, he eased backward to let himself over. His foot found the loop and slipped into it. The cliff was sheer enough so that he had no need to rope his waist and leave his feet and legs free.

"Fare you well, Jarik Blacksword."

Jarik shifted his gaze to Kirrensark. He nodded in a jerk of his head. He gripped the huge knot tied in the whalehide rope as a hand-hold.

He was lowered. He did not look down. The turning in air was unpleasant and he strove to still himself. Once he bumped his hip, with the sound of iron links grating on granitic rock. Once he used his free foot to push himself away from a projection that was hardly a ledge. He was lowered.

It took a long while, and he had time to think many thoughts. Too many thoughts. Few were pleasant.

He looked up to see a couple of faces, staring down at him. The youngster named Coon grinned. Jarik did not. The long broad strip of sealskin that dangled down his back like a cape swiftly conveyed heat to his mail, and in to the padded jack beneath, and through tunic to his skin. A human plumbstone turning, turning at the end of his line. He was lowered.

As he did not look down, reaching the ground came as a surprise. Though his feet came down without a jar, he'd have fallen backward but for his grip on the rope's knot. He remembered to flip the rope. Sending a snaky ripple up it so that those above not only felt the cessation of tension but knew that he was safely down. The cliff rose fifteen or so times his height. It was straight, almost smooth, as if a mountain had been chopped through by the single stroke of the ax of a giant, who had then removed the severed section. From here, at its base and so close to the rocky wall, Jarik could not see the summit.

He unstrapped his shield. While it rested against his leg he buckled his swordbelt around his hips. Slipping his arm through the shield-straps, he turned from the cliffside. The ropes dangled behind him while he set off across the valley.

The temple was larger from here, though not huge, across many paces. He walked, conscious of quiet and wary of uneven ground. Conscious of eyes watching him from the precipice. (*And from the temple?* He banished the thought, and remained wary.) He left his sword sheathed and carried the buckler of wood around its steel boss, thinking on how the longer a man carried such a shield, the more he had to loosen the padded arm-strap; so did the weight of iron-braced wood develop the muscles inside his forearm.

He walked, wary of uneven terrain. He saw insects and few birds. Nothing animal or reptilian. It was as if the valley had been deserted by things that bled and that were green. Nor did he hear any sound of menace; not even the valley's silence was *that* kind of quiet.

He walked surely and purposefully and was careful of where he set his feet, for he knew that a score of men watched. It was not possible for Jarik to walk in a normal manner under such conditions, for he was Jarik, and young.

He reached the temple, and it was *old*. It rose taller than a house, tall as a ship's mast. He saw nothing either inviting or menacing; he saw no one and no animal. A few wasps buzzed, out enjoying sun-warmed flight. Mindful of stones and irregularities of the other terrain, he paced the length of the temple. He walked into the shade at its rear. Emerged into sunlight and walked along the other

side. There, on the south side, he saw the wasps' nests, old
and new, under the overhang of the roof. The roof was
neither wattle nor sod, and he wondered at it. He
remembered that it had gleamed in the sunlight, seen from
the cliff, but he did not think it was metal. He rounded a
third corner of the long building, and was at the temple's
fore.

Walking past the totally unfamiliar architecture of a
colonnaded portico to the corner nearest the far cliff, he
stared up, squinting. The sun was unconcernedly bright
and armor was hot. The other men were up there,
watching. He could not see the rope. Gravity departed his
belly and he swallowed; what if they'd pulled up both
ropes and planned to leave him here? What if they
departed, the moment he entered this gloomy old building
called temple?

"Stupid," he muttered. *We serve the god. They might
desert Jarik, but not Her, and not me so long as I am in
her service*.

He turned back. Paced along before the portico to its
center, where old stone steps led up onto a porch of huge
flat stones set in mortar. There were three steps, and one
was cracked. All were worn and dusty. The dust was not
loose. At least it had gathered and it had rained, since last
people came here—and the ground was dry.

Proud of such observations, Jarik continued to study
the building's face.

A row of nine columns marched across the porch. Each
was the foremost of a file of three. A sword might have
been used in their spacing, for they were about that
distance apart. Jarik stood before and between the fourth
and fifth. The entry beyond them was slightly off-center, a
fact that might have—or have had—meaning. It held
none for Jarik of the Black Sword. The gods were on the
earth, and they lived. In Oceanside of Akkharia, he had
but heard of the gods: the Fog Lords. In Blackiron and
then in Kirrensark-wark he had seen the gods, four in all.
They lived high up mountains, and inside. He knew, for

he had been transported—without walking or being able
to see whether he flew—into the keep of the Iron Lords.
Then, only three days later, into that of their sister of the
Snowmist. The gods were on the earth, and in each wark
were the Three who spoke for them. There were no
temples. There was no specific form of worship. In a way
the people of Lokusta and of Akkharia worshiped Shralla
of the sun and her bereaved lover Serames, and Bodmor
and the Gem Lady, who ruled the night she spangled with
her jewels whilst Shralla slept and the golden glow of her
chariot gave way to the pallid silver of the moon. In a way
these were worshiped, but without temples or priesthood.

There were gods on the earth, and religion as religion
was unborn.

Jarik gazed for the first time on a temple, and he
wondered if once it had been the home of a living god.

He saw little. A building fronted by a porch reached by
three steps, and roofed on a support of seven-and-twenty
columns. (Those mismatched pillars, several newer than
others, were of ironwood, he saw, not stone. And they
were square. This he observed without surprise, for never
either had he seen a building of stone.) At the rear of the
porch, perhaps twice the length of his body from where he
stood, the face of the temple was shaded. He saw an
undoored arch, dark, and only darkness beyond. No
windows pierced the temple of Osyr. He assumed that it
had not been heated, even in winter. (*Had not been,* rather
than *was not,* because he also assumed that it was empty
and long unused.)

(In that, he was wrong.)

Automatically tugging his sword up out of its sheath
and letting it ease back, he set foot on the first step. He
brought up his other foot. Paused. Ascended to the
second step, and the third, and onto the porch. He passed
between the columns and into the dimness of the
doorway's arch.

There he paused, staring about within. Automatically
his left arm moved his shield into a proper defensive

position while his knees bent, just a little. The skin stirred on his nape and a trickle of sweat seemed to run *up* his back. Within, the temple of Osyr was dim. But not in black darkness. There were candles, and they were alight.

Jarik stood where he was, letting his pupils widen to afford him better vision. He narrowed his eyes and did not look at the candles, though those little flickerspots of light in darkness sought to attract his attention. His gaze roved the temple's interior. More square columns rose, to brace huge squared beams. He could not deduce the meaning or purpose of the runners lying across the floor, for a total lack of reference point placed lines of kneeling devotees beyond his imagination. A center aisle broke the crosswise lines. It led forward from where he stood to a blocky altar of stone and wood studded with bronze and copper braces, twelve or fifteen paces away.

Not far enough, he reflected. *A room lies behind the altar, then.*

He moved a step into the temple and a step rightward. With his eyes better accustomed to the dimness, he had become tardily aware of being limned in the entry. Now his shield was between him and it, should someone enter.

Candles burned here. Someone had lit the candles, which though large did not burn forever. (Or could they, in the house of a god on the earth?) Though he had seen no one and heard no one and left the only footprints in the dust on the steps, Jarik felt the chances were excellent that he was not now alone in the temple of Osyr.

In the space behind the altar, perhaps. Guards? A guard?

Osyr. Atop the altar rose and spread a strange sculpture.

A ball of what appeared to be pure gold—gilded lesser metal, surely; the thing was the size of his head—stood a man's height above the two-step dais, on a slender rod of black. (Iron? The god-metal, like his sword; the Sword?) Other, more slender rods stood like rays out from the (solar?) sphere. On the end of each was a much smaller ball. A yellow-white one was nearest the gold sphere. A blue-green one next. A blue-and-white one. A red one. Two, side by side and identical: they were black. Fifth from the central sphere was a very large yellow-green one. Then a strange object, a sphere bisected by a disk. It reminded Jarik of a helmeted head. And four others.

Nor was that the end of the structure. From the blue-and-white sphere jutted an even more slender rod of black, short, capped with a silver ball no larger than a finger-ring. Two such stood out from the fourth sphere, the red one, and others sprouted whole clusters, just as the huge central sphere did.

Interesting. Handsome. Valuable, perhaps—as much for the stalks of god-metal—if such they were—as for the gems and precious metals. Otherwise, to Jarik Black-sword, the structure was entirely meaningless.

Osyr. Osyr stood to the right of the configuration; to Jarik's left.

A glance outside showed him nothing save a passing wasp. It was that kind of warm day, though the air within the temple was cooler. Jarik paced into the temple— quietly, never straightening his knees fully yet not shuffling. He kept his gaze fixed on the black statue. A candle burned beside each of its feet and two stood forth in brackets from the wall, at its shoulders. They lit it, and the light did strange things to the statue. It was of black material—but other colors were there, as if from within, fleetingly revealed in the flickering of the candles.

Jarik assumed that this was a standing likeness of Osyr. And he marveled, while his stomach churned and his armpits prickled. He knew that he had seen this slender man with his thin and aristocratic face. In a vision! Two visions. This was the Guide! His guide into that shadow-realm, that vertiginous realm, that horror-realm of colliding worlds.

A little breeze fluttered through the temple. The two black balls, fifth out from the golden sphere, knocked together. Excitement leaped through Jarik and he

glanced that way. Only the breeze, he realized. He
returned his attention to the statue.

"You came to me twice, Osyr, Guide," Jarik whispered.
"This time I have come to yourself." Even muttering to a
statue, he used the respectful god-pronoun.

The image was life-size, showing Osyr to be not so tall
as Jarik, nor so muscular; his build was lean, endo-
morphic. His face was smooth but his chin jutted a beard,
slim and plaited, no wider than two fingers and little
longer than Jarik's longest finger. Each arm hung straight
to the elbow, where each bent. One seemed to flaunt or
proffer a bush, bearing fruit. The other hand held a staff
about two feet long. It was crooked at the top. Statue,
bush, and fruit were black: a smooth, refulgent black that
glinted with other hues, greens and browns, in the
changing light. The eyes, enlarged and staring, were of a
normal color that seemed strange against black. They
were blue. Sapphires, perhaps, or large round perisines.
Osyr's diadem was surely of gold. Beaten gold forming a
serpent with a strange flat head of a sort Jarik had never
seen. Osyr's genitals were outsized and, like the rod he
held, standing vertical.

The wand, the Rod of Osyr for which the Lady of the
Snowmist had sent Jarik so far, was an off-white. It was
not part of the statue.

A white wand, Jarik mused, touching the hilt of the
Black Sword.

Jarik swallowed, and looked at the other statue.

Also black, it stood on the other side of the altar, to
Jarik's right. The statue was of a woman. It wore a
headdress of feathers—real feathers, tall and white. A sort
of cowl concealed the face save for mouth and chin. It was
a small chin, neither heroic nor god-like. One hand hung
at her side. The other held a long slim rod of black metal.
For the candles, Jarik assumed.

(Do I know this? How?)

Stones that Jarik assumed were rubies tipped the
statue's breasts, which were bare, shining, and pushy. A

fan of three more feathers, down-turned, covered what were apparently hairless loins. A serpent sign, resembling the god's headdress, was coiled on her stomach in a raised design; cameo, circling the intagliated navel.

Black god with gold and blue and white. Black she-god or attendant (priest?) with red and white—and gold. The female statue wore a golden anklet to which was attached a chain of large links. Many links coiled serpentinely at her bare feet. The toenails gleamed red as the gemstones serving her for nipples.

Osyr's mate, Jarik thought, without assuming. Or perhaps his servant. Did gods have mates? Snowmist and the Iron Lords did not—or seemed not to have. Jarik knew that in truth he knew little of those gods on the earth. He knew nothing of this god Osyr, although he'd seen him twice before, in visions. There were many gods.

He wondered. Why cover her loins? Certainly Osyr's were not covered—and enviable, for the man had not been born who did not wonder, and compare, and envy. Surely both statues, she with her fine erect maiden's chest and Osyr holding a fruitful bush above exaggerated genitals in excitation; surely these were fertility figures.

Again Jarik looked all about. Caution was become his surname. And the word for that was wisdom, for *someone* tended this temple that from outside seemed so unkempt. *Someone* kept the candles alight, and fetched new ones. *Someone* tended the feathers on the female statue or idol. Someone came here. Someone might be here now; in the room he supposed to be behind the altar, perhaps.

He heard no sound and saw no hint of movement.

Jarik looked again at Osyr. Eyes on the statue, on its wand, Jarik advanced one step. And jerked violently. At his single buskinned footfall, so careful and quiet, a gong sounded loudly. It reverberated and reverberated echoically in the temple's windowless dimness.

"Hie swiftly from here, O man," the voice said, "else you be dead out of time."

5

Python and Pythoness

"The weavers demand that no man accept life. That is not the choice; one must accept life, and living. The only choice is how."

The warning had issued from a female throat. Jarik froze in a semi-crouch while his eyes searched the temple. He saw no one.

Yes he did; the breast of the female statue moved. She was breathing!

Despite his speeded heartbeat and prickly nape, he remembered and realized: he had no signal from the Bands of Snowmist, which the Lady of the Snowmist had said would grow cold when danger threatened. He spoke without moving.

"How long is that golden chain that binds you, maiden?"

With sinuous grace she stepped from her pedestal. He saw that she was a woman and no more. No god. She had been painted to resemble a piece of statuary. What lunacy! Apparently, too, she had been given some training, for he was sure she had not breathed earlier, while he was studying her.

"I am the Pythoness," she said, and in the same controlled though girlish voice, "Bride and servant of

Osyr. The chain allows me the freedom of the temple. Such freedom is not yours, O man. Depart!"

Jarik understood her though her accent was unlike his. He thought she lied about the length of the chain; his bracers gave him no warning. "How cruel, to paint you and chain you here in the dark to this god of cold stone, bride and servant of Osyr! But I cannot leave you as you demand. She who sent me will not allow it. I shall die else."

"You shall die if you stay. Go, else you be dead out of time." And she moved again, pointing to the doorway with her long staff of black iron.

"May I not visit the great god Osyr, now I am here?"

"No *man* may! Begone. Osyr's patience grows thin. Your presence here is (word he did not know)."

He assumed the term he did not understand was "intolerable" or "forbidden" or worse, and realized that their language was the same but had changed, through long years of separation. *Only a girl*, he mused. *Chained, and bearing a staff too long and heavy to wield well. Nor is she constructed for fighting, this girl of no muscle and almost no waist!* And the bracers remained normal.

Still without drawing his sword, Jarik kept his gaze on the Pythoness while he moved forward. Toward Osyr. He took two steps and she turned and inserted the end of her long rod into a niche beside the black base of the pedestal she had quitted. She turned the rod. It squeaked.

Stone grated on stone. The pedestal moved. Somehow counterbalanced but locked to be released only by her iron staff, it grated aside. Out slithered a serpent. Its colors were copper and bronze and beige below; its head was not snake-flat but strangely ridged. The rippling body that emerged and emerged from its den behind the stone was thick as Jarik's thigh. The head was nigh the size of his own. Slanted, pallid eyes stared at him. The forked tongue flickered as if tasting the air.

In truth the reptile was not gigantic, as it appeared to Jarik. It was just that he had seen none of its ilk before.

Nor did it belong here. The temple of the god was guarded not only by a Pythoness, but by a python as well.

Jarik doubted Snowmist's word—which he had reason to doubt anyhow. His bracers remained neither warm nor cold. Yet he could not believe there was no danger in such a mighty snake! Scintillant, rustling, it rippled and rolled out of its den with an obscene sinuousness. He saw that it was considerably longer than he was tall. Considerably.

Its tongue continued to move with a swiftness rivaling that of a hummingbird's wing. Its unblinking eyes kept their gaze fixed on him, on his eyes. It moved toward him. Sinuous loops of muscle sheathed in copper and bronze. Blight the bracers! Jarik reached across his belly—slowly. Slowly he drew the Black Sword from its sheath.

The bracers chilled.

Pythoness and python stared at the interloper. Gently, with a horrid and horripilating slowness, the serpent arranged itself almost into a pair of linked circles: 8. It stared at Jarik. He stared at its eyes. And then it hurled itself forward in thick ropy coils.

Jarik saw a whipping body like a cable thick as a ship's mast, saw well developed teeth. Saw coils building in the body as it slammed into his left leg. It was not striking to bite, but to enwrap! He was whipping his sword down at the creature, not so fast as it, but it knocked him off balance and the blow was wasted. The Black Sword slashed resistless and bloodless air. Jarik, already astagger, half-spun with the force of the missed stroke.

His leg was squeezed. The pressure leaped up until he was held as no man could have held him. A glance told him that a bulgy loop of serpentine muscle enveloped the leg while another was whipping at him like a thrown rope of gigantic proportion. He struck at that second coil with his sword. At the same time he rammed his shield-edge down at the coil about his leg.

The creature seemed to fold aside with the blow, so that his sword's edge, sharper than sharp, did not slash into it. The shield's edge blow, forcible enough to break a strong man's wrist, seemed not to discommode or discompose his attacker. Frustrated in a twinned attack, hurting, Jarik started to panic. He flailed. Stamped. Tried to move while dragging the snake's great weight. He had no idea that such a creature had strangled oxen in the field, though even that mouth with its fantastic elasticity could not quite stretch to accommodate such a meal. Longer than he, he'd thought—the thing was three or four times as long!

It squeezed, reared, looped, and tried for his other leg.

Jarik's experience with serpents was almost nonexistent. He'd slain one in the garden, once, and been sternly reprimanded. The snake, black and about his present length though not even as thick as his wrist, was a mouser, he was told. On another occasion he'd slain two with two strokes of a sword, in a cave he and Torsy had wanted for the night. He did not like snakes and knew no one who did. His confrontations with attacking serpents was nil, and he knew nothing of constrictors of potential meals larger than rodents.

This . . . thing . . . what was a python, anyhow?

A killer. A leg crusher. A creature somehow able to flip itself in the way of a desperate man trying to snare a foe with coils of cable. And those teeth—but it did not try to bite.

Jarik staggered, struck, banged into a squared column of ironwood, struck, grunted and panted, flailed, kicked; bashed with his shield, which had gone light in his desperation—indeed, in his terror. Staring, soundless and inexorable, the great snake strove to bind him with a body that seemed to consist of nothing but muscle.

The snake thumped against the column. Jarik's standing against it was accident; fortuitous circumstance. The snake's trying to encircle both him and the pillar was its doom. Jarik lurched away, turning. He struck with all his strength and the added force of his spinning half around.

The Black Sword clove through the reptile and

chopped into the column. A reflexive twitch nigh crushed Jarik's leg and made him cry out even while the serpent fell to the temple floor, heavily, in two pieces. Blood so dark it approached blackness spattered as the two halves writhed and flailed. The coil left him. With that leg tingling as though he'd long sat on it, Jarik staggered away. He watched the snake lash and twist, in two pieces.

It had to be dead. It was cleft in twain. It kept moving, though surely dead.

Was it true that dead reptiles did not stop moving until after sundown? So Jarik had heard; that they were beloved of Bodmor who tried to help them appeal to Shralla's sympathy. Jarik had heard that and had neither proof nor disproof. The moving halves of giant snake splashed more blood. Dark blood ran from the blade of the Black Sword as water runs off oil. The blade was not oiled. Such was a property of the Sword, which Jarik had noted before.

Jarik was panting and his heart slammed hard. He'd gone wet with sweat, though his exertions had not been so great. Experimentally though not quite rationally, he chopped off the last two feet of the twisting, writhing snake's rearward position. Warily, he squatted to take hold of—

He jerked back his hand from the section of python.

This snake was not just cold, as were all members of its breed. It was hard; it was *metal*.

Slowly, Jarik rose, staring down at his slain attacker. Why... why the copper-and-bronze scales were not just so *colored*; the reptile *was* scaled with metal, though of flesh and blood. An armored serpent! Only the Black Sword could have slain this creature of sorcery, Jarik realized. And Milady of the Snowmist must know so.

Why... I am important. To Her!

And the less pleasant thought followed: *So long as I have the Black Sword of the Iron Lords...!*

Slowly Jarik lifted his head. His blue eyes were glacier-cold as they glared at the statue-imitating woman called Pythoness—who fell to her knees. She looked down, away from his gaze. He saw that the feathers above her head were attached to a full coif, which was black.

"Why?" Jarik asked.

"It is—it was my duty. I am the Pythoness. I am (unintelligible). It is my duty to serve the god, to keep aflame his licht. To protect his temple."

"That I knew before. Why do you kneel, now? Because I have overcome the god's protector?" Sweat tickled its way down his spine, and Jarik tried to ignore it.

Without looking up to meet his eyes, she shook her head. The white feathers stirred. "You have done what no other has done—you have slain the sacred python of Osyr."

"That is what I said." Jarik stood tall.

She hadn't done: "Now thunder and lichtning will come, for Osyr will destroy us both."

Jarik felt those words as fingers of fear. Yet... He glanced at the statue. It stood as it had before. It was only a statue. Osyr was the dead god. Jarik swallowed in nervousness even while he assured himself that he had nothing to fear from a statue that was only that: an image carved of black stone.

As for the snake—Jarik could well believe and understand that no other had slain such a guardian. Or likely would, were there more of them. Without the Black Sword, he must surely have died. A normal blade would likely have slid from those scales of metal, or at least never halved the serpent at a stroke! The blade of another sword might well have broken.

Snowmist sent me for the Rod of Osyr because I have the Black Sword. Only I could have done this, then. Too, she had tested me. I met her attackers and fought, without knowing they were illusions. I did not flee or fall down weak with fear. I am important!

The bracers were neither warm nor cold and his head was light with elation.

He and the kneeling Pythoness waited. Jarik's attitude

was not one of expectation, as hers was, and he fought
back natural apprehension. The temperature of the
bracers did not change. Nothing happened. The sundered
python's lashing subsided to twitches that Jarik was sure
would not cease until the sun went down. That he
believed. He did not believe that a dead god would send
thunder and lightning out of a sunny sky, to destroy a
man and a woman in a dim old temple.

At last, mindful of his importance and of passing time,
Jarik strode past the slumped young woman on her knees.
He approached the statue of her god. Easily he drew the
white rod from a stone hand smooth as black ice. The
hand was molded into a circle to hold the staff. It looked
silly without it. Only a statue. As for the staff; it was
smooth, cool. White. Like the stuff of walrus tusks,
though he'd never seen one long enough to yield a straight
wand two feet long. Well, a god's staff should be made
from the ivory of the grandfather of walruses!

The bracers were neither warm nor cold. Jarik knew
now that they worked as Snowmist had told him. He had
been warned of danger.

After an instant's thought he decided to thrust the rod
into his sheath and keep his sword in hand. White Wand
of god in sheath; Black Sword of gods in fist. Most
interesting. He reflected. Wondered briefly why the Lady
of the Snowmist wanted the White Rod. She wore pale
grey and silver and white; perhaps the staff had been hers
to begin with? Perhaps Jarik stole from a god who had
been a thief. He did not know. It was not immediately
important, though it was more than pleasant to know that
he was important. So many years trying!

But he was supposed to have slain Karahshisar:
Snowmist.

He turned back to the pythoness. On her knees still, she
had half turned to watch him.

"You see that neither the Sacred Python nor even Osyr
the God has power over me, Pythoness. Nor has Osyr sent
thunder and 'lichtning' to slay you. Why? Wonder! As for

me—I came only for this, the god's staff. I am sorry I was
forced to slay your pretty little pet. Would you have
watched while it encircled and ate me? Have you watched
such spectacles before? Have other men come? Do
metal-scaled serpents eat? Does a heartless statue-
imitating 'pythoness' eat? Now, whilst you reflect that
there may be falseness in your beliefs, I depart as I
came—girl."

She rose. She did not speak. Nor was she broken. She
rushed, two-handedly swinging five feet of slim iron rod
as if it were ax or stave.

Jarik was unprepared for such an attack. Jarik was
also Jarik, and *acatir*, man of weapons, and he trusted no
one—and his reflexes were fast. With a great ringing clang
the Black Sword swept to meet the sweep of her stave.
Sparks flew—as did two feet of the rod, sheared through.
That length whistled past Jarik to bang off the wall,
rebound to clang off a pillar, rebound to ring again and
again on the temple floor.

Even as he had struck to meet her stroke, Jarik had
stepped aside. The Pythoness's momentum carried her
past. Secured to the pedestal on the far side of the altar,
the golden chain sprang taut. Osyr's human guardian fell
with a splat of flesh and a clang of the stub of her staff.
Her mouth oozed a sick grunt.

Jarik took two steps and set the point of his sword
between her shoulderblades. Behind, she was naked from
nape to heel. There was only the thin band that supported
the three white feathers in front. She lay on them. Jarik
was aroused.

"If I lean on the sword, O Pythoness, you die. Let go
the iron rod."

She wept. Her body quaked, and Jarik's body
responded perversely.

"Slay me!" she begged, the words mutilated because
her face was against the floor. "I have failed in my duty! I
must be slain!"

Jarik moved the point of his sword down the line of her

vertebrae and between two hills. "If I lean on the sword, you will know agony now—and pain and anguish all your days, for you will be powerless not to aggravate your own wound. *Release the rod.* Open your fingers!"

She did. She lay sobbing while he toed the truncated rod away. It rolled several feet, while he gazed down at the Pythoness's bare, quake-rippling back. She lay still, tested and found wanting, failed, weeping in despair. He sheathed his sword. Took a backward step, still gazing down upon her.

Well, he mused, *I do have the White Rod of Osyr... and I was not told not to take something for myself!*

He used his dagger to cut a strip from the sealskin he had brought for wrapping the wand. That he now did, that she might not have to see its whiteness and be reminded of his theft. He knelt beside her. The prone young woman limply allowed her arms to be drawn back. He bound her wrists swiftly, not so as to give her pain, and turned her over. Some of the black stain on her skin came off on his hands. She gasped and shrank when he pulled the cowl of feathers off her head.

She was fairer of skin than he—naturally, chained far from the door in this windowless place! She was quite pretty—though her skull was naked, shining and strangely vulnerable in appearance—shaven!

So was she under those other feathers, and sealed more than any other maiden. Long, long ago some monster had sewn her shut! Over the years the skin, perhaps scraped before being stitched, had joined. How horrid that he was both repelled and perversely attracted!

"Only a monster would do this to anyone," he muttered, and he did not like the little quaver he heard in his voice. "And now... only a monster would try to open you."

She stared up at him, a bound victim of incipient religion. Her strange cat-green eyes were like those of a frightened doe. She shrank when he touched her, and he learned with shock that the rubies were somehow bonded to the halves of her bosom! Flashing faceted crests of scarlet. Jarik shook his head.

"Why is your skin dyed?"

"It . . . it is the god. You saw the statue. It is black. His Pythoness must also be black."

"Oh. But that's only a statue. Someone chose—or found some convenient black stone, that's all."

"Obsidian. Yes . . . but who dares say it may not be the true color of the Lord Osyr?"

"Umm. I see. Not I. So. The god's own servant . . . I too serve a god, and she too is cruel—see? These bracers are bonded to my wrists as those rubies are to your breast. But I am not sealed against the way of a man and a woman! I will tell you that I intended to take you, the god's own servant. Don't look so; I will not. I am none so cruel as those who did these things to you. Instead—huh! This serpent on your belly—it is a *scar*, part of the skin!"

"Of course. Tiny knife cuts are made, and aggravated to heal so, in a ridge. Any design can be made thus."

Jarik shook his head. What he did then he'd have denied came from pity. It was in truth perverse. Deliberately, patiently, he stroked the mewling, sweating, writhing maiden through two climaxes. It was hardly the way of a man of Lokusta; it was hardly Jarik's way. He did it, and was proud. He knew need, who had known gnawing need all his life.

He straightened from her, who no longer writhed or twitched but was limp. Her eyes were soft green puddles and she moaned in quiet sighs. Only the most bestial rapist could truly make her a woman, Jarik thought. He had shown her part of what it was about. He was disgusted. Not by her; those who had done all this to her disgusted him. Giving Osyr a scowling look as he passed, Jarik went to her pedestal.

The Black Sword cut anything, and gold was no hard metal. At a stroke he sliced through her golden tether at

the link by which it joined the iron ring in the pedestal. He
returned to her. She hardly flinched when, with care, he
severed the chain from the band—also gold—about her
ankle. He rose and sheathed his sword. He smiled down at
the golden chain snaking across the floor. It was attached
to nothing, now, and it was fully a dozen feet long. A fine
personal reward, he thought smiling, for his simple little
task for Her!

He squatted beside the Pythoness.

"What is your name?"

Her voice was very soft: "The Pythoness."

"You have no other name?"

"I remember none."

"Hail and blight! How long have you been here?"

"I am not sure."

"How old were you when... have you always been
here?"

"No. I was trained from birt', to be Pythoness. I was
brockt here in my tent' year. It was to be when I was
twelve, but the Pythoness before me... died."

"This life is enough to make a woman kill herself!"

The Pythoness, young and pretty and well-shaped,
bald and sealed, decoratively scarred and gemstone-
bonded, looked away. "She did."

"Umm. You don't know how long ago that was, when
you were ten and came here?"

"No," she whispered, gazing at Osyr while she lay on
her back. "Years. Perhaps ten, perhaps less. I know not. It
never mattered."

He did not know why he decided to tell her, quietly: "I
have what I came for. A god on the earth sent me here.
She is alive, armored and masked, and she lives inside a
great mountain, so high up only she can reach her keep.
She is no statue, but alive. She binds me to her service by
means of these bracers. If I try to refuse or disobey, they
give me unbearable pain. She is the Lady of the
Snowmist. She is kith of other gods—the Iron Lords.

Perhaps she is sister to Osyr, too. Or was. Her true name and the true names of the Iron Lords, though, are much longer."

"It is said that once Osyr's name was much longer."

"Umm. She sent me here to fetch the White Rod from the hand of the statue. I must return it to her—far over the water—or suffer the unsufferable. Now I shall also take the chain that bound you—for myself."

"It is heavy."

"I am strong. Besides, I can drag it."

"It does not matter now. I have failed."

Jarik heard himself say uncharacteristically, "I have failed many times."

"Why—why have you told me these things? Reasons, explanations?"

He looked down at her. He blinked, and pursed his lips, and sought his mind for explanation of his making explanations. At last he said, "I cannot say. I don't know. I wanted to . . . I wanted you to know, Pythoness."

He touched her cheek. Then he turned her on her side, with gentleness. He freed her arms, and bound that strip of sealskin around the wrapped parcel that was the White Rod. And he stood up, the wrapped rod in his belt and one end of the chain in his hand. He looked at her for a time, and at last, having found nothing to say, Jarik turned to leave her with whom he felt more in common than anyone, ever. He took three paces, with the chain clinking behind him.

"You are . . . leaving me?"

He only glanced back. "Of course."

"What—what is to become of me?"

He did not like that question. How was it that a few words could force a man to feel responsible when he was not? He turned only half around, so that he was in arrested motion, still on his way out; this way his commitment remained to departure, not to her.

"Who set you here, as shackled minister to the inexistent needs of a cold statue of stone?"

"The Guardians of Osyr. My people; those of Queen Osyrrain, mother of the present Queen Osyrrain."

"Daughter of Osyrrain, eh? So long indeed! Perhaps the queen slew herself too, hmm? And you were trained since birth—is this post hereditary?"

"What?"

"Are you the daughter of the previous Pythoness?"

That concept, apparently, was mildly amusing to her. "No!"

He did not want to ask, but the words came anyhow: "What will befall you now?"

"Death."

"What?"

"Death. I have failed in my duties. The Guardians will slay me." Her voice was tiny, and contained a fatalistic shrug of acceptance.

"The Guardians are warriors?"

"Oh, *yes!*"

"Flee."

Her eyes showed helplessness. "Where?"

Jarik compressed his lips while he stood gazing at her. Reflecting on her and her life. On him, on cruelty and their two fates. He dropped the chain. He drew sword and chopped off nine links, each thick as his little finger but longer, and the swordcut left a narrow fissure in the floor of Osyr's violated temple. He sheathed the sword. Picking up the shorter piece of chain, Jarik went to her, and beckoned.

Her eyes sought some sign from him as she rose. He swung the length of golden chain about her waist, several clinking pounds of gold, and hooked the links together. He had cut carefully, and the chain lay on her hips, tugging at the linking so that it would hold. A sectioned link contained two hooks.

He returned to pick up the other length. It was heavy. He wrapped it around his waist anyhow, more than twice, and secured it.

Then he held out a hand to the Pythoness, confused

and unhappy young warrior to confused and unhappy young priestess. "Come."

She looked wide-eyed at his face, at his hand, at his face. "Wit' you?"

He nodded.

She came to him, naked but for the feathers and the chain and the glittering decor of the rubies. She took his hand. He had replaced her headdress. The three white feathers indeed rose from a full coif, black. The erect feathers stood not quite so high as the apex of his helm.

"Do not look back."

She gazed up at his face, and did not look back.

"If we see aught that menaces, let go my hand at once."

"Your weapon-hand. Yes."

"Come, then. We will think of a name for you—woman."

They left the temple, though she hesitated in the archway.

"I am a woman?"

"Of course you are a woman."

"I am...I am your woman?"

"You are my woman. The Pythoness is dead." *And I am insane! What will I do with this poor sealed creature who knows nothing save this dim old barn peopled with black stone?*

Her hand squeezed his, and they stepped onto the portico. Then, "The sun!"

"Ah! Blight and hail—I'd forgot! The sun will be deadly to you! Have you nothing in there to wear?"

"No-o..." She shook her head.

"No bedding?"

She shook her head. "The stain. Will this stain on my skin not protect me from the sun?"

"Yes—I think." And he wore no cloak!

With a sigh and a rolling of his eyes that was only for himself, he released her hand, retrieved his from it, and unslung his shield. He could not chance it; she might burn to a crisp before they reached the cliff. Perhaps the dyestuff all over her would protect her, and perhaps it would not. He pulled the sealskin parcel from his belt and the links of gold draped heavily over it, and unwrapped the White Rod. With the thong he bound it to his sword-sheath; the hook at one end of the rod would not let it slip free.

She acted as if she did not know what to do, when he proffered the flayed hide of a sea-dog. Jarik swung it around her. He used the strip he had cut from it to fasten it at her throat. It formed a waist-length cape that covered her back, shoulders, and upper arms. She put up a hand to the makeshift clothing, rubbing it as though it were fine fur. And she looked at Jarik with eyes that shone.

"If the sun is in front of us, you will pull that around over your chest and walk behind me, in my shadow. If it is behind us, you will walk before me. If to either side, I and my shield will shade you. Come."

They left the Temple of Osyr.

6

The Guardians of Osyr

The bracers warmed in the sunlight. So did the Pythoness, who at first squinted and averted her face from the skyborne glare she had not seen for the better part of a decade. And then she opened wide her eyes, and cavorted, basking in the light of day both physically and emotionally. Jarik, who had known few, wondered how many happy days she had known in her strange life. Bride of the god, indeed!

Helpless servant of an unappreciative god. As he was.

The sun was to their right now, and Jarik kept her to his left, with the shield between them. Twice he reminded her of how swiftly her skin would burn if the dye proved transparent. He leaped forward to catch her when she danced ahead like a child. A naked worshiper lifting up her hands to the bright glow of Shralla the sky-queen. He drew her back into his shadow. He held her there while they crossed the plain to the cliff. The white feathers nodded above her coif-covered head, and it was easy to forget that she was hairless. She was beautiful. A boy and a girl walked in the sunlight. It was warm.

He saw no one atop the cliff now, but Jarik didn't worry. They would not have deserted him. Jarik Blacksword perhaps; not the servant of Her that he was—until he gained his freedom and returned to his true mission: the death of Her.

64

He asked the Pythoness whether the Guardians did not come to the temple. Of course, she said. And devotees; worshipers? All the Guardians were such, she told him. All her people. She used a word he did not understand, and she questioned a phrase of his. With a gesture, he asked how it was then that no road or trail or even clear path ran from temple to cliff.

"Oh, they don't come from the *cliff*," she told him.

He looked about, trying to spot a trail worn by many feet over many years. "From where, then? By what route?"

She gave him a large-eyed look. "I do not know. I have been in the temple," she reminded him. "And I remember little of . . . before. I think the drug took away some of my memories."

"The drug?"

"Oh yes. I was drugged every time they put the marks of the Pythoness on me, and the herbs were re-administered for several days each time. And of course when they brockt me here—and made me fast with the golden chain." She slapped it where it was slung at her hips, and she almost smiled. "Two of the old God-Women were wit' me, and remained for many days. They gave me the drug daily. When they departed and I was alone, they left a small supply and warned me to take tiny amounts. It was when it ran out that the agony began. Then I knew all—and rats seemed to be clawing at my stomach, from within. I shrieked and writhed and cast myself about. I remember the first time the chain drew me up short, so that I fell and wrenched my ankle. I was miserable."

"And—"

"I became accustomed to it. What are you called?"

"Jarik," he said, and with his new surname on his tongue, he swallowed it and let the name stand alone. Jair-ik. She had seen the Black Sword. She had not seen him with the *morbrin* rage on him. "What is the drug called?"

"Jelmet," she told him, and it was a word meaningless to him. "Jair-ik. Jair-ik?"

"Yes."

And as they walked he discovered that in Kerosyr's changed version of the language they shared, his name had come to mean "Friend of the Sea" rather than "Gift" or "reward" *of* the Sea. His name, he thought, while she tried to dance while his hand gripped hers, and looked all about at a world that was new to her. His name, and she had none.

Though the bracers gave him no indication, he wondered about the danger to them both. "Tell me of the Guardians," he began, but she interrupted, pointing and shouting out in a piping voice hardly proper for the god-servant she had been.

"Ooooh! LOOK! A clin! I *remember*! A *clin*! How *beautiful*!"

He glanced up at the dove and then at her, and Jarik's mouth quirked in a smile.

"The name of a crawling slithering thing will not do for you," Jarik told the Pythoness. "A bird's name would fit you . . . a happy, free-flying clin! Be thou Clinye!"

"Oh, how *nice*! Named for the dove!" Then she made a face. "But not Clin*yeh* . . . Clinain!"

"I only applied the womanly ending to the name of the bird," he said, unable not to feel a little—however ridiculously—hurt.

"Not here, Jair-ik. Not among the Guardians of Osyr! A woman's name ends in *-ain*, and it's a proper name at all!"

"Oh. Well. It is certainly a most proper name for you. Clinain, then. It does seem as strange to me as Clinye seems to you."

"I'm sorry." That was as silly as his feeling a sense of hurt. The young woman looked up at the young man, concerned and nervous. She was more vulnerable than he, he realized. And far more fragile.

Jarik felt very warm toward her, and protective, and

wondered if a man could love a woman who was sealed against him. And—would her hair grow back?

"I'll get used to it," he said, and he smiled and squeezed her hand. They had almost reached the cliff, where the ropes hung awaiting him. "Does your hair grow, Clinain?" It was easier calling her that, since she had no other name for him to force off his lips and out of memory. "The Pythoness" had never been right, Jarik mused.

She lifted a hand that did not quite touch her head, under the skullcap that held the feathers there. "Yes. My scalp has been shaved and, and oiled, lotioned, every . . . every fortnicht, I think it must be. These are your ropes, Jair-ik? You climbed down thus?"

"I was lowered. I am going to tie this chain and the Rod," he said, drawing the sun-warmed links from around his waist, "in this rope. The loop tightens. They will be drawn up. The other loop does not tighten. It's for the foot. Shall I send your . . . belt up with this?"

She touched the strange, heavy girdle he had given her. His gift to her, though unintended; a thief's gift, from the god she had been raised, and trained, and forced to serve.

"May I keep it?"

"Of course," he said. Although he had not intended to give her the two feet of gold chain, he was unable to say so. "Isn't it heavy?"

"Yes—I mean, I feel its weickt. It isn't heavy, Jair-ik."

He knew what she meant. He had given it to her, and it could not be heavy. *We are a pair indeed,* he thought; *two people with the inner needs of ten!* He nodded while he tightened the noose on the god's staff and the long clinking, flashing chain. A glance up the cliff face showed him nothing but cliff. He shouted as he now thought he should have done yards away, when he could see the summit. He tugged the line.

After a moment, with nervousness commencing to build in him, he tugged it again.

Relief welled and made him momentarily weak: the

rope began moving up. They were there, waiting. Jarik stood.

"Now," he said. "My comrades will pull us up. You first, Clinain. Step into this loop, and hold onto the rope just above this big knot—very tightly!" He glanced at her bare feet. "Have you ever worn footgear, Clinain?"

"Clinain, Clinain," she said, making it a song of joy. She hugged herself and the chest-rubies flashed red and fiery orange. "No. Never. I know what you are thinking, for you wear those things on your feet. 'Footgear'—what a strange phrase! The rope will not hurt my feet, Jair-ik. It's just that . . . I will be so warped!"

"What? Warped?"

"Oh." She smiled, brightly. "Afraid, I mean. Your people do not use 'warped' to mean 'afraid'?"

Jarik shook his head, gazing on her with an uncharacteristic and rather silly expression of almost paternal fondness, while a feeling of protectiveness surged in him with physical force.

"I understand. Just hold on tight. You will be safe. Men will draw you up over the top . . ." Jarik frowned. They'd know he sent her, Kirrensark and Delath and the Hounder and the others. She'd be all right, wouldn't she?

Frowning a little, he touched her. "I do have companions. They will not know who you are. Best I go up first, then. You will do as I said, when we let the rope back down for you?"

She met his gaze with hers, and she put her hand on his arm, and nodded.

"I was about to ask you about the Guardians of Osyr," he remembered. "Well, I will once we're out of this valley."

"Jair-ik . . . I am afraid. I have never been out of the temple. I have failed the god and I have abandoned him, and . . . and you have *men* wit' you. Oh, and Jarik—I love you!"

He held her because she wanted to be held, needed to be held. He was not comfortable. Love? He'd only just met her. Had he rescued her, or sundered her from what was meant to be her life? What did "meant to be" mean? Did he feel more than protective toward her, because he was sorry for her? He'd have raped her had *they*, the Guardians, not sealed her. Now she said she loved him. Alye had said that once; no, twice. Alye of Harnstarl. Alye was dead, and so was Torsy, who had loved him and wanted to be more than his sister.

He held Clinain, just born and just named, a bit tighter. Surely his armor hurt her. She did not complain, and he did not think of it. He needed to hold.

He released her, smiled, said, "In moments the loop will return for you. Put one foot in and *hold tight* with both hands!" He stepped into the loop, and tugged. She watched him drawn upward. She looked up at him, fearfully. Sword and shield on back, Jarik Blacksword was drawn up. He held the rope and rested the base of both fists on the big knot. She would have to reach much higher to grip here, he thought. He smiled. Clinain could do it, and she would!

He did not look down. The cliff seemed to move past him, going downward. He knew that the ground, and Clinain, were a body's length away. Two body-lengths. Five to go. And up, and up, turning slightly at the end of the rope. He had as many problems as ever. More. The problems of Kirrensark, and Delath Berserker, and the Lady of the Snowmist. His mission for the Iron Lords. And now the added complication of the Py—of Clinain. Clinain. She was so—

The bracers went chill. They became cold. Jarik gritted his teeth, and was drawn up. He dared look down. Her upturned face looked very far away. Then it vanished beyond the slant of the precipice, and he saw only the feathers, and then nothing of her. The bracers were cold. He had been drawn up too far to allow him to jump, and too far to fall. The Bands of Snowmist coldly promised danger and he could neither escape it nor, at the end of a rope held by what he presumed was the source of the danger, meet it properly. He was being drawn up to it. The danger itself was drawing him up. The bracers were cold.

Kirrensark and company—had they turned on him? The Guardians? Then where was *Seadancer*'s crew?

Senseless to speculate. How could he meet the promised danger as a man of weapons, as Jarik of the Black Sword, when he dangled at the end of a rope and a fall from it meant death?

Clinging with his left hand, he drew his sword over his left shoulder—with care, and slowly. He rose up and up, cold in both arms. And he looked up.

Eyes stared back into his. Hazel eyes beneath brows and a single white feather rising above a headband of tooled leather.

"Slip that weird black blade back into its sheat', man, or choose: hang there or be dropped."

The pronunciation was different again, but he understood. Almost he let go the rope. He did not. Jarik stared into those strange eyes that were not blue and not grey, the only eye hues he had ever seen.

"The Osyrrain will be interested to see you, defiler." The lips were stained a deep blue-pink, nearly lavender. The hair was like none Jarik had ever seen. The sun struck cerulean and dove's wing grey from its highlights. The hair was blue. Blue as a rainy day.

With great care, slowly because that was necessary, Jarik slid his sword back into its sheath, on his back. "Draw me up," he said. "When I come over the edge, I will be on my belly. You can take the sword then." *Or slay me easily*, he thought, *while I am helpless on my belly with my feet dangling!*

"True. Your cooperation is bot' (unknown word) and intelligent. Pull him up."

And Jarik, his bracers cold, was pulled up into the hands of the Guardians of Osyr, of Kerosyr, and they were all women.

While two looked at him along the shafts of nocked arrows and others stood with drawn swords, Jarik examined his captors. He had nothing else to do; trying to fight or to run would have been fatal.

All were black of brows and blue of hair. All had deep blue-pink lips, as if they had found a way to turn red clover or foxglove into a cosmetic. Surely the hair was dyed. All were naked, save for ornate bow and quiver of arrows, belt for sword and dagger and carry-pouch or wallet. And a headband from which stood a single feather. Three of the women wore each a red feather thus, and the other six wore white ones. A necklace of small shells circled every woman's neck and from it a small bag, grey and furry, dangled in the valley between the breasts. Mouse-skin, Jarik mused. He noted that a breast of each woman was tipped with a ruby, which he assumed was unaccountably bonded as was Clinain's. Each wore a braided leathern cord at the waist with a phallic pendant molded, surely, of silver.

The ages of his captors seemed to range from fifteen or so to mid-twenties or past; it was hard to be sure. All three wearers of the red feather seemed older, and one was pendulous of dugs. All but two of these women seemed shorter than the great majority of the women of Lokusta, and though none was remotely brown, all these Kerosyrans were darker, too.

More sun, Jarik thought, if he thought about it then.

Surely no man had ever been more strangely captured. Though they wore none, his helm and footgear and tunic were not objects of wonder to his captors. He was sure they knew what they were and had seen them before. The Bands of Snowmist were a novelty. Holding him at the odd, right-angled points of their broad swords, they removed his weapons belt. The Black Sword was remarked and remarked upon. The Bands could not be removed. The women—women!—bound his wrists behind him and hobbled his thighs at the knees. He was left able to walk without difficulty—provided he made no attempt to stride out.

While he was being trussed he contrived to use his foot to send the ropes over the precipice. *Don't call out,*

Clinain. Don't call out . . .

"Walk carefully, defiler. Fall going down this hill and you will roll a long way."

"I will have care. I am flattered that you have my weapons, and there are nine of you, and still you've bound me."

"Let me just stick the arrogant stoat, Ershain."

"Hush, silly," their leader said; she who had first spoken to Jarik. "He is tall, and well-formed, and hardly ill-favored. He can be of value."

That, Jarik mused, was nice to know. He said, "Where are your men?"

Several of them laughed, while two scowled. Lavender-mouthed and blue-tressed, every one of them. And naked save for decorations and weapons.

"Oh, we have men, man," the leader said.

He looked at her. "You are Ershain?"

She nodded. "It is this one's name."

Had she said "uh," *one*? He was not certain. Their accent differed, and the usage was unfamiliar to him. He decided to ask.

"Did you say 'one' and not 'I'?"

"One," she said nodding, looking . . . superior. "We have not your arrogance, defiler. We do not say 'I'. One is . . . one. This one is Ershain."

"Ah." He nodded, slowing nothing, or trying. Queer, most queer. No personal pronoun. Arrogance, she called it. *Do they think themselves important only as members of a group? Do they see their sole purpose to be what Clinain called them . . . Guardians?* He had no idea. Clinain called herself "I" but perhaps that was reserved for her closest to the god. Jarik did not know. In truth he had done well, for a young man without experience or referents. Yet with an entirely normal xenophobic chauvinism he thought, *"One" for I! How stupid!*

Ershain gave him a little push. "Walk, defiler. Down the slope."

Jarik walked. Three women went before, sinuously,

and he dared not watch the movement of bare haunches. With his hands bound behind him and his knees separated by a cord only a little longer than his hand, he had to watch the hillside he descended. His desire not to fall was doubled; the second reason was that he did not wish to be anything less than dignified and manly before his captors. Jarik was Jarik, with his needs. And his youth.

Two, one a spear's length behind the other, flanked him on either side, at distance of ten paces. Their bows remained strung. Ershain was immediately behind him. A woman nearing thirty years and wearing a red feather above blue hair. Another followed her, well back.

They distributed themselves as hunters, he thought— or warriors. He assumed the first. Though they were most warlike in appearance, who on their blue-mountained isle had they to fight? Hunter-warriors then, surely.

And what did their men do?

He wanted to know about Kirrensark and the others. He wished he knew whether they had preceded him into captivity. The trouble was, he could not ask. It was possible that they had seen the Guardians coming and decided to depart unseen, to observe the women. Or they might have quit the clifftop before the Kerosyrans came. In that case the presence of these women might be unknown to the Lokustans—whose presence might be unknown to the Guardians.

No, they must know, he decided. There was the evidence of the ropes at the clifftop. Nevertheless these Guardians might well have no notion as to how many men accompanied him . . . if they still did. Best not to ask or mention his companions, Jarik decided, despite his curiosity approaching anxiety. He would know eventually, whether all the crew were dead, or captive, or free on Kerosyr—or fled altogether.

Meanwhile, he walked. In company of martial women with bows excellent in appearance, apparently plated with pieces of bone or horn that flashed white in the sunlight. And they knew how to flank a captive. Without bending from the waist, his captors prowled like predatory cats, limber and without ever completely straightening a knee. They *flowed*.

They reached the base of the long hill without his falling or seriously stumbling. Insects and birds chatted among the woods Jarik and his captors skirted. A yellowish foxglove, nearly as high as his knee, brushed his leg and one of the Kerosyrans picked it. He assumed it was for some purpose, dye or medicine. They skirted the base of a richly grassed hill and entered a wood where there was no trail. No one held aside branches or bushes for Jarik. He would not request or complain. Armored, bound, he plowed through, wading and ducking—and emerged with his guards onto a good worn trail!

He squinted up through the trees. The lacery of leaves dark on their undersurfaces against the pale blue of the sky.

"We've done a good bit of roundward walking to come to this trail," he observed loudly, though in an equable tone and manner. "And we are headed south again, just as we were when we took our first step down that hill."

"You see, Fisheye?" Ershain said, applying a hideous name to a very pretty young woman—the one who'd wanted to stick Jarik. "He has a brain, too."

"Moss knows nort'" Fisheye said, "but one never heard it called intelligent."

"Easy, warrior, easy," Ershain said in a tone with a metallic edge. "One can see to it that this time next mont' you are the only whit feather of your age!"

A couple of women laughed. Jarik was sorry he had spoken. Their bickering taught him nothing, but only confused him. And no one had answered his intimated question anyhow.

"You are right, defiler. This is the trail to our wairk," Ershain said, and he assumed that he heard still another culture's pronunciation of *wark*.

"Trail? There is only one?"

"Aye. Open all the way to wood's edge, above the best harboring place. We do not care who finds their way to us—so long as they come by this one trail. It makes it (unintelligible; "easy"?) for us to be ready."

"Clever. But what if they enter the woods at some other point, and just fight their way through the bush?"

"You will see."

And, in time, he did. They walked along that pathway broad enough for three to walk abreast, and came to a place where another trail intersected. Jarik asked about it. It disappeared swiftly into the trees, curving.

"That insures that all visitors to the wairk follow this path," he was told. "That one completes a great circle in the woods, without ever coming near the wairk. Consider. Men who are as you said fickting their way through the bush would be delickted to come upon an easy route. Whichever way they follow it, it leads to this one."

Clever, he thought, but he asked, "And if they stay in the circular path and go all the way 'round?"

"Then they arrive, eventually, more tired than they mickt have been."

And thus easier prey, he thought. "And if they split up when first they encounter the circle," he said nodding, "they will eventually meet."

"Aye, and know it is a circle. One group will say 'Ah—we passed another trail back there.' And back they all come, and down this trail in a body."

"To die?"

"Eventually. Eventually, defiler."

Jarik walked, watching the backs of the Kerosyrans in front of him.

"You tell me much," he said after a time.

"Yes," Ershain said from behind him.

"I am not to leave your *wairk*, then."

"No," Ershain said.

Jarik walked in silence. His guards talked carelessly, casually.

After a time a whistle shrilled from behind Jarik; it was Ershain. Every one of his captors halted instantly. After a couple of more steps, Jarik did too. He did not turn while behind him Ershain muttered an order. The wood had gone silent. A woman trotted past him. Unusually curly cobalt hair bouncing on her shoulders, which were well padded though her hips were lean. She bore his shield. She contrived to make it stand on edge, propped in the center of the trail up ahead, broadside to the woods on either side. Jarik stared at its edge, wondering.

She returned to Ershain, eyeing Jarik as she passed. While he eyed her.

Ershain whistled again. Two smooth, fluidly connected notes.

A few leaves twitched and deadly bees seemed to hum. From the trees and bush on either side of the trail came whizzing a score of arrows, and two spears. With a staccato rattle fourteen arrows peppered the shield while the boss turned one and another caromed off the ironbound edge. Perhaps others would have struck it too, had not one of the spears knocked it over. Extremely impressed, Jarik reckoned that perhaps only three arrows had been deflected by leaves or twigs—the leafy sounds he'd heard; the others had coursed clear—and one spear must have been miscast. Even so it had driven into the bush beyond the shield.

"I see," Jarik said, when he was sure that his voice would sound normal.

Ershain laughed. So did a few others of his captors. Then, with a minimum of thrashing sounds among the leaves, fourteen women sprang from the trees as if to attack the shield. Ershain whistled, and they froze. Gazing past Jarik at her. That too was impressive, as he assumed they were seeing him for the first time. They were so disciplined as to look right past him, at their leader. He noted that all of these wore a sparse loin-cover, of cloth.

Ershain advanced to Jarik's side and a few eyes

swerved to appraise him. "Retrieve your arrows, Guardians. You who missed, hand yours to Hishain. And—who made that bad spear cast?"

Hangdog of attitude, a white feather Guardian of perhaps sixteen said, "This one, Ershain."

"Noted. Bread duty till morrow zenith; spear practice morrow afternoon; (unintelligible) with Jilain before dinner."

Her gaze on the trail, the youthful Guardian nodded.

"The rest of you: Good shooting!" This time Ershain's whistle was only a single sharp peep, as of a startled bird. There was no way Jarik's eyes could report the movements of all the fourteen ambushers as they returned into the forest. They had vanished in twenty heartbeats, and before his heart had pulsed thirty times more, all sounds of their woods-passage had ceased.

"You used a word unfamiliar to me," Jarik said. "What must she do with 'Hilain before dinner?"

"Hakatuayna," Ershain repeated, and thought for a moment. 'Combat," she said. "A practice passage of arms."

"Oh."

"Is that all, defiler? Oh?" There was laughter.

They were warriors all right, Jarik reflected without pleasure. He'd make wager that bread duty meant the youth had to work at the making of bread all morning. Since that was obviously a punishment, they had a caste-system in which warrior-hunters ranked higher. Then she was to weary herself throwing her spear all afternoon; she was still warrior. He'd also wager that the "Jilain" this Guardian was to work out with, with arms, was one of their best. The instructor, perhaps. Jarik was not eager to see that burly mare—though thus far, of two-and-twenty Kerosyrans, he had seen none fitting such a description. He had seen no bulging bellies or bulging muscles. Ershain was commander, and nearly thirty; Ershain was compact, lean, large only of calf and

buttocks and eyes. Such evidence was unable to pierce the
natural wall of prejudice that shielded the logic center of
Jarik's brain.

He answered: "I think I had rather come here as bound
captive than otherwise."

Laughter. "Is that all, defiler?"

"As I serve a god, who is not Osyr, and was sent here by
Her, I am no defiler. And I have a name."

"Who cares?"

Jarik straightened his mouth and ground his teeth.
Keeping his lips very tight, he said, "Expect no bragging
on your warriors after *that*, Ershain of Kerosyr!"

He was aware of stares, which he affected not to notice.
Gazing straight ahead, he knew that others were looking
at their leader, to see what she might reply or do. *Were
they going to slay me,* Jarik thought, *they'd have done it. I
haven't even been harmed. Therefore someone must want
me brought to their wark, alive.* And he said, "Must we
continue standing here? Am I to be taken to your wark?"

"You are anxious indeed to enter a place from whick
you will never leave, defiler!"

Jarik had taken enough verbal slashing. He turned.
For the first time since they had started down from the
cliff, he faced Ershain and looked into her hazel eyes. *The
eyes of a dog,* he thought, who had seen no eyes that were
not blue or grey and was secure in the prejudice of
ignorance.

"Your tongue is sharp, Ershain. Hakatuayna with this
one before dinner!"

After a few gasps gave way to a wintry sort of silence,
someone chuckled, high-voiced. Ershain controlled
herself and coolly returned Jarik's gaze.

"You are so brave it is danger to you! This one will
request it of the queen, man, defiler of Osyr's *helderen*
temple."

Jarik was surprised and impressed with her, and hard
put not to show it. He did blink. He forced a smile.

"Something to look forward to," he said, and turned and began walking with the odd short paces his thigh-bonds forced. Ershain must either follow or have him stopped, only to order the march resumed anyhow, once she'd proven her point.

He knew she had given a sign when the two advance Kerosyrans wheeled and set off as if leading him. He looked down at his buckler as he passed it. Fourteen arrows had chewed the round shield, and he scowled to see that the outermost strap, the hand-grip set in its inner surface, was broken. The spear-head, he assumed. He walked on, following naked woman, flanked by naked women, wondering why those in the forest wore loin-covers. He heard Ershain pick up the buckler.

"I hope that strap can be repaired before we meet at swords' points," Jarik said without turning.

"Parilain will commence seeing to it the moment we are within the wairk," Ershain told him. "It will be made as good as it ever was."

Jarik smiled, walking. "And how may I depend on that promise, Ershain?"

Abruptly she was beside him. "Listen. The Guardians are not as you—others. Promises are sacred." The word she used was *helderen*, the same she had applied to Osyr's temple. It meant taboo; off-limits to the extent that guards were not necessary. A married woman was *helderen*, and the firstman's seat, and a girl younger than thirteen, and the person of any of the Three, who spoke for the god. That the law would not be broken was taken for granted; that was *helderen*.

All promises would be called *helderen*, a surprised Jarik reflected; few of course were. He glanced at the woman beside him. Ershain looked very sincere indeed. Suddenly he'd have been ready to wager that she meant it. Among those of the Isle of Osyr, a promise was sacred: *helderen*; unbreakable.

He realized that he was staring at the woman who

walked beside him, and that he was frowning. He smoothed his forehead, looked ahead, turned his face back to Ershain.

"I believe you."

She looked surprised. After a time she said, "What is your name?"

"Jarik. Jarik of the Black Sword. I am called Jarik Blacksword."

"Jair-ik karn-starl."

"Yes."

"You are young. And you are no bad man, are you Jair-ik karn-starl?"

She and he had surprised each other again and again. Now she had done it again, and Jarik considered seriously. "I serve gods. I have slain men. Three gods sent me to slay a fourth. I did not, and she sent me here. Either she is evil and a liar, or they are, or all four are. I did not come here willingly; I have no use for the parcel you took from me, your god's staff. I stole the chain of gold for myself. Yet I know him, your god Osyr; I know him as the Guide I have seen in visions. I stole from him." He heaved a sigh, with shocking effect on his pronouncedly developed chest. "I never meant to be, Ershain, but... I think I am a bad man, yes."

"You have talked wit' gods."

"Yes."

"Wit' Osyr?"

"In visions. He spoke to me. He told me... things. He told me of... strange matters, and happenings."

"You are no bad man, Jair-ik. How could you be? You have been visited by Him. And you say these things to this one, openly. You even call yourself bad. No bad person calls herself bad, Jarik Blacksword."

They walked on, with Jarik once again frowning, aswirl within unwelcome thoughts like a ship storm-caught far out to sea.

"One believes that you do not lie," Ershain said quietly.

"Except perhaps when you style yourself bad."

"I lie." Jarik had not even hesitated.

Again they paced in silence. Until she said, "And when you promise, Jarik Blacksword?"

Jarik gave that thought before he answered. "I try hard not to make promises I might not keep, Ershain. I try hard not to break them. But I could not call a promise of mine *helderen.*"

"Your honesty is shocking, Jair-ik. One is sorry that you did what you did, and that one cockt you at it. You are unique, one thinks. Can you believe that among the Guardians, promises *are* sacred?"

"I said that I believe you, Guardian. I do. I cannot conceive of the possibility of people unable to break promises—but I believe you anyhow. You are different. This island; the Guardians—are different. And I do not care for this converse with you."

"The wairk is nigh." She pronounced it *nickh.* "Why not?"

"We are enemies, woman! You call me defiler, and tell me that I will not leave your wark! I tell you that I will, and I will try to leave it alive, and if it is necessary there will be blood on my sword. I tell you that my life is more valuable to me than anything. Anything. You are my enemy. I do not care to talk with you, to know you, man or woman. Let me lay hand to hilt, and tell me again that I cannot leave your wark alive, and I will splash your blood. I have no care to get to know you, commander of Guardians."

She was silent for a long while, and they walked, and ahead rose a wall of tall thick poles. They were straight trees past the sapling stage and thicker than thighs, and laboriously, multiply lashed together. Laced together, all tight-pressed. A walled wark, he thought, with some wonder. In the middle of a forest!

"Yes," Ershain said as they neared the tall palisade. "It would be terrible for us to discover that not only do you and this one respect each the other—as we have, and do!—but that we like each the other as well, wouldn't it?"

Jarik heard, and frowned. He said no more while they walked the last paces to the wall of upright poles behind which lay her wark—"wairk."

7

Osyrrain

The Black Sword neither bends nor nicks nor will it break,
nor rust nor even lose its edge. It is yours. You took it up,
and used it. It will not leave you, Jarik. It is yours.
　　　　　　　　—The Lady of the Snowmist

The buildings were all of wood, which was familiar
enough to Jarik. That all rose well above the ground; that
the roofs of thatch were oddly peaked to form an angle
like a dagger's edge; that all were tall and well separated;
these were unfamiliar phenomena. Nor did these people
of Kerosyr connect their homes with a system of planking
on thick supporting posts, so that snow could be hurled
off and leave walkways, and so that when the snow melted
one need not slop about in the muck. That was the way of
northern Lokusta, but not of Kerosyr. And one structure
here was more huge than the house of a firstman of
Lokusta. Jarik saw that it was almost a replica of the
temple, save that there were windows and not so many
pillars.

They paced toward that building, that great house.
Captive and captors. The people of the village took note,
yet not as he might have expected.

They are used to seeing captives brought in, he
thought, and knew that he was wrong. *No. Something*

*else has distracted them this day. Taken the edge off their
natural curiosity. I am just one more captive.* Thus by
logic he did not realize was extraordinary did he decide
that Kirrensark and the others of *Seadancer* were all here.
All, unless some had been slain.

Fronted and backed by erectly gliding women, flanked
by them, Jarik entered the fifth wark or village ever he had
seen. And this was the most different.

The constant banging grinding sounds were not from
the two women methodically pounding grain, he
discovered. They were loud enough, those two older than
his captives and nearly as naked; both wore red-squirrel's
tails over their loins, pendent from plaited thongs about
their hips. Most of the racket emanated from one
meaty-armed Kerosyran who was large of chest though
small of breasts.

She was pounding two large rubies and several chunks
of feldspar into a powder. To be mixed with urine and a
bit of avian blood, Ershain told him when he asked. It was
a medicine.

Jarik did not ask what it cured or healed. Thus these
islanders spent beautiful gemstones! On nipples as
permanent decoration, and in medicine. Strange, strange
people, with their women acting as weaponers.

That reminded him, and he glanced around. Where
were their men? Their *boys*, even?

He saw none. He saw a potter's apprentice painting a
small two-handed jar, and she was female. He assumed
that she was apprentice, since she was so young. Beside
the just-nubile girl, her mistress was using a slender needle
of flint to incise a design on a similarly painted pot. After
the vessel's final firing, the design would appear in black
against the red color. The design was not simple.

Without registering the knowledge, Jarik saw that
other, finished pots were more handsome than any made
by any people he knew. Since the woman wore a single red
feather above her brow and her apprentice a white, he
wondered if that were the meaning of the two colors.

Something to do with maturity, then, he mused, doubtless awarded in some Kerosyrish rite of passage. He did notice, with surprise, that the girl did not so much as glance up at the passage of him and his escort. He remembered the discipline of those warriors of the wood. Yet the potter or artist, a woman of perhaps forty, did pause to look at him. She stared. Glanced at her assistant. Stared again at Jarik. He passed, concentrating on looking tall and cool, stalwart and brave.

He did not feel all that brave. He was a captive of foreigners, and he was guilty of invading the temple of their god—and robbing it. No; he was the foreigner! For this was their isle and he was an invader. Territoriality was theirs, and strengthened them. He was the foreigner. That made it worse, and Jarik concentrated on looking braver than he felt.

He and his escort paced toward the greathouse.

Before it stood Osyr. Ten feet tall and well carved of a single piece of hard wood, darkly stained. This workmanship was not so fine as that of the statue in the temple; this one was thin, tall, straight, a stylized phallic line short on detail. While this representation of the god also proffered the fruited bush, its other hand held no wand or rod, but a sword. Back there in the temple he had invaded stood fertile god-Osyr to greet his devotees; here in the wark to greet captives and encourage the Guardians was militant war-leader Osyr.

The statue in the temple is older, Jarik mused. *These Guardians did not make it. This one they wrought, much later. Great artisans made the first.*

Just before the statue there was a platform of shining wood; on it rested a low-backed chair of dark wood decorated with plaques of horn and a bit of gold. The chair had but one arm, the left. Pelts covered the ceremonial seat, fox and young marten or winter weasel, in a handsome pattern of white decorated with red. The tails hung across the front of the seat in a thick furry fringe, each white one ending in a black tip.

The firstman's seat, Jarik Blacksword thought.

He was halted several paces in front of it. No words were spoken. A woman of forty or more, wearing a garment of fur around her hips and what appeared to be a normal enough cloak over her upper body, looked him up and down. Then she turned and went into the big building behind throne and statue.

"See that the strap of this shield is made better than it was," Ershain said, and a Guardian went away with Jarik's buckler.

He met Ershain's eyes, then glanced around. He saw only woman and children, and few of those. Several of the children were entirely naked, and Jarik saw that they were girls. As for the women—Guardians they might be, but certainly all were not warriors! Several had achieved advanced age, and had pots below the navel, though no one here was truly fat. Two stringy old women, featherless, sat crosslegged on mats, side by side. Their loins were covered and he decided that perhaps was a mark of age. Were the loins of older women less pretty? He did not know; Jarik had never seen any. From a few feet away these two stared at him, and all the while they solemnly chewed lengths of leather to make it supple.

Good binding cord, he thought sardonically.

Another oldster, apparently supervising both cookpots while tending neither, was no chewer of leather or anything else. She had no teeth. She wore a big bone ladle in her girdle, like a sword. A chief cook who could not eat!

Here then was a complete wark, village—with no males in sight. What did they do, the men of Kerosyr? Two youthful white feathers sat facing each other. Sharpening swords with daggers lying beside, they shot him glances from time to time. Otherwise—something else strange. Save for the very very young, he saw no other white feathers.

Ershain spoke a single word and the word was unknown to Jarik. Immediately her squad formed two

lines that created between them a broad aisle from their
captive to the throne. He waited. A glance at the two aged
softeners of leather showed Jarik one of Ershain's
warriors squatting with them. The weaponer had his
shield, and indicated it while she talked to attentive
women. One nodded and reached for the buckler. She
looked up at him. For an instant Jarik essayed to look
pleasant. Then he again glanced at the throne and the
statue rising behind and above it.

The cloaked, fur-skirted woman had emerged from the
big building. She paced with solemn dignity out to the
throne to take up an obviously formalized position to its
right. She stood on the ground, not the dais. She wore no
feathers. Jarik wondered what the firstman would wear,
now his woman had presumably advised him of the
presence of a captive requiring his attention.

Jarik had no experience to prepare him for the fact, or
enable him even to consider it: There was no firstman, in
the wark of the Guardians of Kerosyr.

From the greathouse now came another. A woman.
She walked straight and unbending with gliding steps so
that only her feet and head moved. That head was held
high, confident of self and role and superiority.

This woman of less than thirty years was too lean, even
of face, to be pretty. Neither was Kirrensark handsome;
such was not a requisite for command. Her chin was
pointed and her mouth small between gaunt cheeks, and
her nose long and thin with tiny pinched wings. And she
was thin all the way down. Yet she was handsome, this
woman, because of the way she carried herself.

About her blue-tressed head coiled the serpent sign of
Osyr, in gold. Its eyes were yellow gemstones and above it
lofted two white feathers. Another was fastened to point
downward over her loins, and it was not quite adequate to
cover her. Jarik saw no sign of hair below this woman's
eyes. Her bosom was bare of rubies as was no other breast
among the Guardians. Instead, a gem flashed like frozen
blood from her forehead. Jarik was sure that it was

bonded there, and he assumed that the gems were set in place when these people were very young, and that only painful bloody cutting would get them free. That was inconceivable, which led him to wonder about the dead. Was there somewhere on Kerosyr a burial ground rich with rubies? The red gems were obviously tribe-signs. Culture symbols, probably not seen by Kerosyrans as jewelry at all.

This woman—who held a short slim staff of gold, a fruited bush—wore a single piece of jewelry. A huge chunk of red gold circled her upper left arm. It was carved with the face of Osyr. Its eyes were sapphires. She was otherwise naked, wearing not even so much as a ring or torc or amulet.

Walking straight as an animated reed in a beautiful though affected gait, seeming to see no one, she ascended to the dais by means of an unseen step at its rear. Jarik watched her step past the fur-covered chair, sidestep to be in front of it. She sat. Her knees were together. Her eyes remained fixed straight ahead all the while; the first-woman among the Guardians knew where her dais and seat were, and woe to any who happed to leave any obstacle in her way!

*No one sees the bare backside of the firstwoman— first*woman—*of the Guardians,* Jarik supposed, and wondered how she departed. But he was being silly, and knew it.

The woman who had gone for her, who alone among the Guardians wore clothing, now stood beside the throne. She spoke, loudly to the wark at large.

"Behold the Osyrrain, who speaks for the god." After a moment of silence, she said, "Ershain."

Ershain went forward. She spoke low. Showed her ruler the golden chain and the White Wand of Osyr. Shocked, Osyrrain would not touch them. She looked at Jarik and she too was lavender of lip and blue of hair and brown of large eyes surrounded by brown cosmetic so that they seemed huge, and to stare dramatically.

"What of the Pythoness?"

"She strove diligently to protect temple and god," Jarik said, thinking with some sadness, with a qualm of guilt, that he had not truly freed "Clinain" at all. "She bade me begone. I would not go, and I advanced. She released the serpent."

"She did release the serpent? But—you are here."

Jarik nodded. "I killed it."

Kerosyrans were gathering now, and he heard gasps at his words. They did not mutter; the clothed woman was staring about. Bound, Jarik stood straight and made his brain work for him. A thought came, another; they formed an idea. Perhaps he could impress them unto overwhelming.

"*Killed*—you k—*how*?"

"With my sword. I am Jarik of the Black Sword," he said, hoping by the phrase to instill more awe. Obviously that he had slain the serpent was considered impossible and therefore not credible, and therefore more than impressive. He heard murmurs and saw the Osyrrain's aide glare about. Silence returned on the instant.

"The Black Sword is the gift of gods," he said. "It cuts what I want it to cut." *Oh yes, Ershain*, he thought, *I do lie*. For he assumed that anyone who wielded the Black Sword would cut anything he wished. Or she wished!

"Where is this black sword?"

Ershain took Jarik's weapon to the seated ruler, who looked at the sheathed weapon without touching it. "Well, well, draw the swoord, Ershain. Let one see what it—*black*! A black blade!"

"Aye, Osyrrain," Ershain said. "Hence his name."

"Once one passes sixteen summers, Ershain, one should have learned to cease stating the obvious. So." Osyrrain looked past her warrior at Jarik. "You slew the *helderen* serpent of Osyr."

"With my helderen sword," Jarik said.

"You will not be impertinent, defiler of the temple!"

Jarik saw that the ruler's eyes brightened and seemed almost to flame. And he had heard her slash of sarcasm at Ershain. A most high and proudly mighty woman, this chief of the Guardians!

|"I meant no impertinence. The Black Sword is a gift of gods, the Iron Lords whose names are Destruction, and Annihilation, and Dread. Now it is peculiarly mine. The Sword is helderen." That, he thought, was mere exaggeration, not lie.

The queen waved a hand impatiently. It was strange, that her fingers and wrists were bare of gems or precious metals, she who was Elye mah-Elye: Lady of Ladies among the Guardians.

"You slew the serpent."

"I did. I left it in two pieces."

Jarik heard gasps and murmurs. People had gathered, though he did not turn his head to look. The squad of Ershain stood in their two lines, in position to splash Jarik's blood should he lunge at their ruler.

"And the Pythoness? Did you moorder her as well?"

Jarik let pass the imputation that he had "murdered" the great reptile. "I did not. Once I had slain the snake, she too sought my blood. She wielded her rod of black iron. The Sword sheared through it." (He heard muttering.) "As the chain shows, she is no longer in bondage to a man of stone. And I showed her what a man of flesh and bone is like."

"The Pythoness is sealed against men!"

"Aye, and so she is still."

Ershain, near the ruler, had turned to look with horror at Jarik.

"Clarjain!" Osyrrain said. "Take four and fetch the Pythoness here! Do not walk!"

While the squad of four left the wark at a trot, Osyrrain gazed at Jarik. It seemed to him that she stared, studying, thinking, rather than glared. Certainly others were glaring, including her cloak- and fur-wearing aide.

"You are a mickty warrior," Osyrrain said. "Others

have come here. Some fled at the gong and command of the Pythoness. Those who were not so sensible were soon slain by the Python of Osyr. You have robbed us of the Python, defiled the temple and the very person of the Pythoness, and stolen from great Osyr himself."

"And great Osyr did nothing," Jarik dared remind her. "My Sword is powerful; my god is powerful. It is obvious that her power is greater than that of Osyr. Best you release me and let me be on my way about my business."

"Not likely! Osyr will—her? You said her?"

"Aye."

"You spoke of the Iron Lords, with names chosen to strike fear into the heads of little girls. Who is this 'her'?"

"The Lady of the Snowmist, their kith." And Jarik told the queen of the Guardians about Snowmist, and of his quest.

"Why does this female god of a far cold land want the Whit Rod of Osyr?"

"I do not know, Lady of Ladies. She—"

"Call one Osyrrain, foreigner!"

Jarik showed her what could have been a nod or a little bow of his head only. He would not bow verbally; he would not bother to tell her that he had sought to address her respectfully. He said, "She wants the White Rod, Osyrrain. Surely Osyr is—was of her kith. Perhaps she wants it as a remembrance. *She* is *alive*. Osyr does nothing with it."

"You are bound, a captive, and unarmed. You are (unintelligible adverb) foolish, Jarik Blacksword. Doubtless you think 'foolish' and 'brave' are the same. It is the way of *men*, isn't it? Osyr *will* act, throokh this one. The Pythoness has merely proven herself unworthy. Her successor will not be so. You are very alone, Jarik Blacksword."

Jarik said nothing, but met her dark-eyed gaze. He saw her lips move and push up her cheeks very slightly in a mere hint of smile.

"Doubtless you now think on your companions,

foreigner. Oh, we know of them. But you *are* alone. You
are captive. Your fellows are even now enjoying
(unintelligible) and the companionship of maidens of the
whit feather. Thus do all men who come here and do not
flee the temple to their sea-craft—or die in the temple.
They are doing what you could be doing, but for your
sacrilegious deeds."

Jarik's stomach went empty. His heartbeat speeded
and his legs were mere saplings trying to bend beneath his
weight. They had Kirrensark and the others, were plying
them with girls and—that word, which he took to name
some strong drink they made here.

And revelation had come on Jarik. He said,
"You ... have no ... men."

"Wrong."

"There are no men here!"

"Oh but there are! Those who accompanied you here,
Jarik the Defiler!"

"I saw no boy-children, only girls ... you have no men!
The Guardians are all women—this is a wark of women
only!"

"We are the Guardians of Osyr, alone with him on this
isle," Osyrrain said, gazing levelly at him. Serene and
supremely confident and superior. A ruler beyond any
Jarik had seen, among mortals. "Osyr demands that we be
women, only."

Jarik said slowly, "I see." His throat was dry. "So you
use the men. Those who come here, by whatever means."

"By whatever means? Oh, it is always by the sea that
surrounds us, Jarik Blacksword. Only twice have men
come here other than by sea-craft, ships, and each of them
was alone. One had fallen off a ship in a storm; the other
survived when his ship sank."

"And you use them."

"Of course. Else there would have been no more
Guardians, longer than long ago."

"Then your actions are baser than mine, with the
Pythoness. And the children from such matings?"

"The girl-babies are raised to become Guardians of Osyr. When one has eyes of the hue of amythol or amygnant, she is groomed as Pythoness."

Jarik felt cold. At the same time, his armpits prickled with sweat. *Gods! ye gods: could I be of these people? Am I an abandoned boy-child of Kerosyr?*

"And the boys...they are...slain?"

Osyrrain's gesture was casual, deprecating. "We have no need or want of men, and thus not of boy-babes. Osyr has forbidden us to keep them."

Jarik spoke with his lips tight. His words were brittle. They were stones that he flung at Osyrrain, though in a quiet, almost dull tone. "Ah. You have much blood on your hands, Osyrrain, as I have. We are worthy of each other, we slim young killers!"

Ershain and the aide glowered at him; their ruler stared with bright eyes become smoldering coals. Recklessly Jarik went on:

"Those white feather maidens with my companions...on the morrow they will begin to wear the red feather?" And when she nodded, Jarik said, "Remove my bonds then and we will remove your white feather, my fellow killer!"

While her people expressed shock, the ruler greatly surprised Jarik by pointing, ordering his bonds removed. Now while reason flooded over him, for he had gone almost *morbrin* in words, slashing with words, he wondered that she did not order his blood splashed.

Ershain herself effected the command, slicing the cords with her dagger without care for the cutting of the bonds into his skin. She had whistled, low. Two women covered Jarik with their handsome double-curved bows. The queen's eyes were bright.

"Remove your metal coat."

Jarik did. Getting it up onto his back and then upending to shake and wiggle the chaincoat down into a pile of links, while the Kerosyrans laughed at a man with his head and hands down and his rump in the air. The underjack of padded leather, Osyrrain bade next, and Jarik removed it. He heard the mutters, the sibilants. He stood tall, in sweat-darkened homespun tunic over leather leggings, drawstrung. Striped arrows pointed at him. Ershain stood close, and her sword was in her hand, not her sheath. Jarik looked to their queen.

"The tunic," she said, and he removed it. He stood consciously tall, conscious of their eyes, and he pushed out his bared chest. Almost, he was smiling. "Bind his hands in front of him."

"Bind—in front—" He moved in jerks, but the arrows were nocked, pulled on tight strings.

He subsided and submitted. She had called him "mighty warrior" and stared so at him; surely she was taking him at his word, and would have her white feather removed by him who stood up to her. Why these bonds, then? *But she specified my hands be bound in front of me,* he mused, again approaching the mood for smiling, *to protect her from me but to be able to get my hands on her*!

When the strip of three braided pieces of hide had been wrapped twice around his wrists, and each end pushed through between them, and drawn around and twice knotted so that there was no chance of his freeing himself, he looked expectantly at Osyrrain.

"You dared make the suggestion of supreme arrogance and insult, defiler and idolator, not this one. Osyrrain would not consider such, and be soiled thereby. This one promised that Osyr will act, throokh me. Osyr will. Osyr demands," she said more loudly, rising, "that you be whipped!"

Betrayed and stricken, Jarik started to move. His bonds held, biting his wrists—and he was tripped. Jarik sprawled. His legs were held, at the ankles—by feet planted on them. Women surrounded them. Warriors stood over him. He lay helpless, surrounded by none but enemies. The points of nocked arrows seemed to stare at him. A tensing of his arms assured him that he'd accomplished naught save cut his wrists on the braided leathern thong.

Putting out a hand that was instantly taken from beneath by her aide, Osyrrain stepped lithely off the dais. Her gaze was on the sprawled captive. She did not frown, or even smile; Osyrrain smirked.

Jarik decided. He was bound and downed and surrounded. He could not save himself and the gods he served were manifestly not going to do. No use struggling or striving. *I am going to be beaten.* He set about steeling body and mind to be beaten.

My hands blistered and popped and I was embarrassed, mortified when that wrenched a groan from me. What agony that was! I was eight, and thought I had to be a man. I will take care of you, Torsy. I got to be a man. I'm the man and I got to take care of you! And, at eight, he thrust his hand, bleeding from the oar, into the salt water. And he did not scream.

Now he did not see the lash that was brought to the ruler of the Guardians. He did not care to see it. He heard it. A nasty *wheep* in the air, and then a loud slapping noise and a blow. A flash of pain took possession of his back. He felt her draw the whip back, slowly, so that it slithered from his bared skin in the manner of a serpent. He clenched his teeth and breathed hard through his nose, inhaled hard through his nose.

The evil whine of leather in air again; the loud crack-slap noise again; the fire of agony again.

Jarik bore it. His mind was in the grip of a web of iron of his own forging, and he withstood the pain. He wanted to cry out, to yell, to scream. He did not. *No man is so merciless as a woman.* He had heard that. She was striking hard, very hard, putting her body into it. He moaned a little, and was not happy about it. He wanted them to see no sign, to hear nothing from him. Let them see how a man behaved; let them see how Jarik took pain! He wondered if the whip was peeling his back. It felt so.

Yet he was not aware of any tickly trickling sensation, as of blood. *Uh!* It *hurt!* Crawling off him again, only to come leaping back to bite, this new serpent of Osyr. His body had become acutely alive, aware of every sensation. He felt the stir of air. He heard the whine and Osyrrain's gasp of exertion and the snapping slap of the whip; he heard the gasps and occasional murmurs of the onlooking Kerosyrans, and he smelled them, smelled their odors; smelled their sweat and his own. His brain, locked in iron, tingled with exaggerated life despite his efforts to dull it and he was agonizingly certain that all could smell the odors of fear and pain that filled his own nostrils.

Fear, yes. For no man is made of iron and no brain caged in iron, and the whip *hurt*.

A particularly severe lash brought a "*hunh*" from Osyrrain and a similar sound in a different tone from Jarik, and then the whip fell no more.

His back felt as if someone had been rubbing it with nettles and he did not want to move for a long, long time.

"Oil," a voice said, and it was not Osyrrain's voice.

"He shall have no oil," a voice said, and it was Osyrrain.

"Oil," the first voice repeated, and nearby he heard Ershain say, "The Moon-Mother decrees oil for his back," and not without pain Jarik turned his head to see that this Moon-Mother was the clothed woman, who he had thought was aide to Osyrrain. Somehow among them her word was higher. He assumed that she spoke not often, that the ruler might rule. The Moon-Mother must be like unto the Three among the warks of Lokusta, who spoke for the god and advised the firstman of each wark. Revered old women who otherwise said less than little and held respect thereby.

He prepared himself by gritting his teeth. He heard the footsteps. It was poured on him, and it was cold. It hurt. Oil. He knew that it would be good for his back. Just now, though, it was not welcome; it was cold and it hurt. Better they had all spat on him, for anyone knew saliva had curative powers.

"Stand him up." Osyrrain's voice sounded even more angry than before, now she had been overruled by the Moon-Mother.

Hands laid hold of his upper arms and he winced at the grip on a welt. He was tugged up, and he ground his teeth that he might not scream, for his back screamed in pain. His back creaked and stung from the movement of welted skin over muscles perhaps bruised. The oil ran down. It wormed its way past the waistband and drawstring of his leathern leggings, and it was cold and not pleasant in the crack of his backside.

They turned him to face the queen. Her eyes were intensely bright. She no longer held the whip, he saw, but had her hand fisted around the hilt of the Black Sword. He saw a sheen of sweat on her arms and chest. He noted too that the sun was rapidly disappearing from a sky going grey as his mood. He supposed that she had not bloodied him and his senses and his mind remained intensely keen. Jarik shook off the grey as a great dog shakes off rain, and he calculated.

"Wit' your own sword one shall slice away that which defiled the Pythoness, and then your brazen head!"

"The Pythoness," he said, "remains sealed."

Osyrrain said nothing, though some of her people muttered. Jarik forced his voice to remain low, his tone to mimic calm.

"The Black Sword is mine, Osyrrain. It will not cut me."

He had no such knowledge and indeed would take vow that it was not so. But the bracers were not cold, and his mind was working well, and he knew he had opportunity to save himself. Nevertheless Osyrrain said nothing. She clutched the Sword and glowered, and advanced a pace on him.

"Bid them cut me loose, Guardian of Guardians, and I

will show you the power of the Lady of the Snowmist and the Iron Lords—and of Jarik Blacksword." He added, "I make promise and vow that I will not use it against you."

"*Promise*!" Osyrrain spat. "We know what value men place on promises! The promises of your kind are boar's teeth that have bitten us aforenow!"

"Ring me with spears, then," Jarik said. He strove not to sound desperate. The bracers had not gone cold. Were they failing? Had Snowmist left him? He was about to lose his manhood, and the bracers pretended that he was in no danger.

Then I am not. I am capable of removing it. How? I have only my brain, And my mouth.

He had given her pause, made her to pause, glaring. Though she sneered, he saw that she was fascinated. He remembered no scene more tense in his life. What could he say now? Just release me . . . ring me with spears . . . let me show you . . . let me get my hands on the Sword . . .

There came a little flutter of wings and the faintest humming little moan. Down into Guardian-wark as if from nowhere flew a dove white as a cloud on the clearest of days. It lit, precariously, on the shoulder of the captive. It did not preen or behave as a bird, but appeared to stare at Osyrrain. In her surprise the ruler blinked several times rapidly, and backed a pace. Though he was scarcely less shaken than the queen and her people who buzzed like bees in quest of a new home, Jarik turned his head and spoke as though accustomed to such a phenomenon:

"My Lady!"

The lovely bird, so sleek and so soft looking, twitched its head to stare into Jarik's eyes. Then it leaped aloft. It flew away, and some idiot loosed an arrow at it. Too late. It missed. The dove vanished among the trees surrounding the wark as if it were a bird of green rather than of white.

Those who had muttered spoke aloud their wonder now, and Jarik stared at a stricken Osyrrain. He tried to

look knowing. Menacing. She sneered to cover her
nervousness—and ordered him ringed about with spears.

Soon eleven Kerosyrans had formed a circle to aim
eleven spears at him. Eleven rubies gleamed dully from
the tips of otherwise bare breasts. Eleven feathers nodded
above sapphire hair. And eleven pairs of eyes stared at
Jarik, inimically. The spears were held two-handed, and
low. Their tips were but inches from his body.

"Release him," Osyrrain said, and it was done.

8

The Defender of Osyr

Bared to the waist, he moved his arms slowly, gingerly, wincing at the call upon strained muscles and the tugging at skin already stretched in welts.

"Would you please let go my Sword?" Jarik said, with an almost courtly politeness.

Osyrrain blinked, frowned, stared at him, glanced down at the Sword she held.

"Humor the helpless captive, beaten and surrounded by leveled spears," he said, and two or three Guardians snickered. "Keep the Sword, but only set its point against the ground and open your hand."

Visibly wondering and just as obviously not overly happy about any of this, Osyrrain did as he asked.

The Black Sword immediately rose straight up, so that had she closed her hand it would have been about the blade. It tilted then, and—avoiding two spear-wielders with seeming care—moved to Jarik at a speed approximating his own stride. The eleven Guardians moved restlessly and their knuckles paled on their spear-grips while they watched Jarik's hand close around the leather-wrapped hilt. Spearpoints wavered, ready to transpierce him.

Jarik thrust the blade into the ground beside his leg, and folded his arms across his chest. The Black Sword stood beside him like a dog at heel. The Guardians stared in silence, too astonished and awed even to murmur. Osyr had wrought them no such miracle as a homing sword. Those well back tiptoed and cocked their heads this way and that to see over or around their fellow.

"Hold," Osyrrain bade the eleven guards.

"The Black Sword is mine, Guardian of Guardians. It remains with me. Give me my weapons belt, and I will sheathe it."

"He is a god!" someone said.

That emboldened Ershain to say, "He says that Osyr has spoken with him..." and another asked, "Are you a wizard?"

"Only a captive encircled by sharp spears. My I sheathe my Sword?"

"Give him the belt," Osyrrain said, and Jarik was glad that she possessed curiosity.

Ershain handed him his weapons belt with its pendent sheaths. All three were empty. He drew the Black Sword from the earth, wiped it on his legging, and slid it into its sheath. From behind her Guardians with their leveled spears, Osyyrain put forth a hand.

"Bring this one the belt."

The Kerosyran who reached for the belt watched Jarik's eyes warily. He released the belt with no other movement. She backed away still staring into his eyes, glancing nervously at the red hilt of the Sword. She put the broad, thick belt into the hands of her ruler. When the Black Sword began to emerge from its sheath like a serpent from its lair, Osyrrain dropped belt and all.

The Sword returned to Jarik. Again he grounded it beside his foot.

Mine, he thought, with exultation soaring in him like an eagle. *It is mine! It returns to me in the manner of a good dog to its master! And look at Osyrrain; look upon Jarik, you Guardians of a dead god! For I am the agent of living ones, and my Sword will not stay from me!*

He had no idea as to the nature of power of the dove. A sending of the Lady of the Snowmist, he surmised. He was not even certain he knew the full power of the Sword from the huge skystone in Harnstarl; what else might it do? Certainly he did not understand it. Only that it was his, and invincible and unbreakable, and that it would not stay from his side. He did know that the moment was his. Now was the time to strike, through a bluff.

The Bands of Snowmist were normal in temperature; his back had gone chilly.

"O Guardian of the Osyr Guardians," he began," it is time for you to—"

The interruption was most unfortuitous. Into the wark and to this central court area came five Guardians, and with them was she who had been the Pythoness; she Jarik had named Clinain... Dove.

Kerosyrans moved aside, and Jarik no longer had the full attention of anyone, including his encircling guards. The former Pythoness was hustled roughly—and unnecessarily—through the crowd and dumped to her knees before Osyrrain.

Osyrrain asked several questions of her who had fetched the Pythoness. Clarjain advised that the Pythoness was still sealed. At that news Kerosyrans muttered and glanced at Jarik. The Pythoness had been at the base of the cliff, weeping. More questions brought confirmation of what Ershain and Jarik had told Osyrrain—and the shameful news that the bride of the god had had great pleasure of the foreigner.

Osyrrain showed more fury than horror. "Rise then, bitch in heat, and watch him DIE, pierced by many spears!"

"*No!*" Clinain cried, and flexed to her feet.

She spun and began to make for Jarik, shoving, and behind her the red-feathered Clarjain, all in one smooth warrior's motion, drew her sword and thrust it into the bare back of the Pythoness.

Jarik saw the stricken look on Clinain's face, saw her gaping mouth and bulging eyes, and he saw the point of Clarjain's broad thick sword when it emerged in blood from Clinain's belly. And Jarik stopped seeing, and thinking.

Jarik's hand snatched up the Black Sword and his left hand hurled backward the nearest of his guards whose spear-butt slammed into the thigh of another, who cried out and fell while Jarik's body slammed itself past another leveled spear in the hands of a distracted guard. Without a sound, Clinain had dropped to her knees, sliding off the smeared and dripping sword in Clarjain's hand. Clarjain watched the Pythoness topple forward, loose-armed and limp of neck, and Clarjain looked up at the rushing man an instant before the Black Sword came humming around in a blow so horribly, insanely forceful that it sent her head flying aspin. While the headless body still stood fountaining blood, Jarik's body was swinging away, not hearing the cries of those in the path of the flying head who squealed and ducked or dodged and were spattered with the blood that was a scarlet pinwheel around the spinning head.

By the time they could focus their gazes again, Jarik was behind Osyrrain. He twisted her arm behind her while he held the Black Sword in a grim horizontal line across her throat. Clarjain's blood ran from its blade in the manner of water gliding off oiled leather or a duck's feathers. It dribbled down Osyrrain's chest to form a necklace of garnets. She shrank—against the captor behind her.

Every Guardian froze. Their ruler's face was the color of snow and her eyes were great brown pieces of glass.

"Monsters! I gave that girl the only pleasure of all her life! What say had she, when she was forced to be bride of a statue? What say had she, when her head was shaved and she was chained forever in that gloomy barn of a temple after being *sewn shut* to make sure she never pleasured herself as you pigs must do, day and night? Monsters! Servants of a monster queen! Get back! Back, back. Go and fetch my companions or I'll slice open this cow's throat—slowly!"

While he glowered at them from behind their ruler and over the feathered head of their ruler, Kerosyrans were thrust aside from behind. A warrior bullied forward. She was erect and more than twenty though not yet thirty, and her red feather that waved as she advanced stood higher than most. She cleared the others and stood before them to stare at Jarik past the terrified face of her ruler.

Jarik stared in return. Tallish she was, slim, marvelously shaped with superb musculature gliding smoothly as a cat's beneath smooth skin the color of doehide and unpadded by the hint of fat. Her deep-blue hair was cropped short so that her ears showed, and the back of her neck, under that small sapphire cap like violet-highlighted feathers of jet. Hers was a gymnast's body, an athlete's body. Hers was a firm-mouthed face neither homely nor beautiful. The blood-hued gemstone of the Guardians flashed from the outermost curve of her right breast. Eyes the color of Ershain's stared at Jarik's; pale brown eyes. *Dog's eyes*, Jarik thought who had never before today seen eyes colored other than blue or grey; *but gods, O gods but she is magnificant!*

"Release the Osyrrain," she told him, in a voice that was at once entirely feminine and that rang with the authority of confidence. "Meet this one wit' that sword, *man!*"

Her own sword was naked in her hand, and she bore a buckler, a circle slightly flattened into a gentle oval like a cabochon.

"I will fight no woman," Jarik said, and arrogantly added, "much less a girl!"

"This," Osyrrain said in a tight voice, mindful of the blade at her throat, "is Jilain, best warrior in the memory of Kerosyr!"

"Ah," Jarik said, remembering the name. "Guardians who do not well are ordered to spar with her at arms, for punishment. Well, I have *been* punished."

He spoke over the confusion he felt, as he felt the loss of

his advantage. *Blight* this wench, tallish among her people but hardly any sort of opponent for Jarik of the Black Sword!

"No one appointed you to punish Clarjain!" Jilain snapped.

"I heard no one appoint her murderer of the Pythoness, either—who had never harmed anyone. Be away, else—"

"Refuse to fight this one and you will *die*," Jilain told him, "for she—he—who would not fight an armed *woman* once the battle-lust leaves him would not slit the throat of an *unarmed* one—boy!"

Still the startled Jarik held the ruler's arm with his left hand; still he held the Black Sword high and horizontal, at her throat; still he gazed upon the doubly handsome warrior of Kerosyr. And he knew that she was right. Yet still he could not agree to meet her in combat as if she were a man.

Jarik nearly died, then. The red feather warrior did not share his bias or his compunctions. She did have the confidence to act on her convictions.

With Osyrrain between her and Jarik, Jilain attacked. Her sword was aimed for his left side, which was exposed beyond the slim ruler. And Jarik realized at that instant that she was right. He had no battle rage on him, and he could not slit the throat of the helpless woman he held. His hand quivered while he reminded himself that she had whipped him, meant to unman and slay him. But no, he could not kill her this way.

On the other hand, it would be easy to shift her into the path of Jilain's stroke...

Jarik could not do that either, though now he had to take instant action—or be chopped. At the last possible moment he swung his right arm out from Osyrrain, straight out so that the Black Sword was a kill-sharp plane rushing at his attacker's chest. He was sure she could not stop, or hurl herself aside, and there was no time for her to interpose her buckler. She would be slashed deeply, and soon Jarik would have Kirrensark and the others out here...

Jilain's buckler blurred into line to catch his blow with a bang of metal on heat-hardened wood, and Jarik knew he faced the fastest warrior he had ever seen. Desperately he thrust Osyrrain from him, under his extended right arm. She stumbled rightward and two of her spearwomen were able to come alive and move fast enough to prevent her falling asprawl.

His hastily devised tactic had failed. His attacker was unharmed and he no longer had his hostage. Jarik had to hurl himself back from the sword stroke Jilain directed at him. Her point rushed past his chest, and had he worn clothing the sharpened iron would have scraped it. Once she had missed, he beat at her blade with his, hoping to strike hard enough to hurt her arm or knock the slender Kerosyran off balance. That failed, too, for she moved with the stroke. Twisting, she interposed her buckler to block his raking backswing. Though the Kerosyran sword was single-edged and thick on the unsharpened edge, apparently used for chopping the Guardians' ways through the woods and perhaps for collecting small wood for fires, it was capable of being wielded in a backswing. All Jilain did was twist her wrist and bring her arm rushing back. Once again Jarik had to resort to his legs, dodging away.

She was not only fast, he realized; the Kerosyran was better than good!

A woman!

"No!" she suddenly shouted, looking past him. "No one must touch him! This one is champion, and this one makes champion's promise that none will touch him wit' hand or blade until he and this one have settled our fickt!" And she cut at Jarik, who ducked, bumping into a Guardian who stumbled aside. "Osyrrain?"

"Aye," the ruler called, her voice sounding small after

the ring of Jilain's. "It is promised. He is *helderen* until Jilain is finished with him. Slice the bloody barbarian to strips and morsels, Jilain!"

And she calls me *bloody*, Jarik thought. But—*Good! At least I won't be stabbed from behind while I try to find a way to—while I easily defeat this mere stripling female* warrior!

Each of them had advantages and disadvantages having nothing to do with gender. The Kerosyran had shield and iron sword while Jarik had no shield and was no expert at sword-to-sword defense. That was what a shield was for. Men did not cultivate the science of meeting blade with blade. On the other hand, he wielded the Black Sword, a better weapon than hers or any other. She was naked—and accustomed to her nudity. He, conditioned to relying upon his mail in combat, was bare above the waist. Still he reminded himself that he gained a bit of speed and maneuverability without the weight of the chaincoat. He would need such mobility, with her so swift and him without shield or mail for defense! Already he had made the unencouraging discovery that the odd Kerosyran blade was not so easily broken or chopped through as those he was accustomed to. The Guardians' single-edged blades were thicker, broader, and less likely to snap near the shorter, single-edged and therefore less delicate point. He had his height, and certainly both his strength and that of his weapon exceeded his opponent's.

I'd be better with an ax, he thought, *against a shield*—and he laid hold of his hilt with both hands. He was going to have to avoid her blade while he chopped her shield to bits. She was too fast for him to believe he'd easily get over or around it.

She struck. He backstepped and parried and struck. She caught that slash on her shield and cut low and he chopped even while he sidestepped precipitately. No blood flowed, and her shield-arm held. They began to circle. Crouching and watching. Bam and clang; his stroke was met by shield and he had to yank the blade to the side to intercept her counter-stroke. And circle, crouching, watching.

No one interfered. The Guardians watched while their best warrior fought the defiler who had slain the Python of Osyr, and Clarjain—and indirectly, the Pythoness. He must die. Jilain would see to it.

Jarik cursed his pride and wondered if it would slay him. It was pride that prevented his raising a clamor about unfair fight since he had no shield. Too easy for them to reply in sneers, pointing to his height and his "mickty" build and longer reach. No, he'd not bring that on even to save his life. He'd find a way. If her sword could withstand his blows, surely her buckler could not—or her arm.

The two circled, warily watching each other. Now and again muscles tensed while he feinted, or she; when the defense was there and ready, that attack was aborted. She feinted with her eyes and slashed high in an upward-looping cut he avoided only by going straight down into a squat. Somehow her shield leaped between her leg and his chop at it. Wild two-handed slashes kept her at bay while he got himself fully vertical again.

The dance went on, the death dance of two strong good warriors watching for an opening, any opening, any weakness. Any opportunity to hurt, or wound, or worse. The other Kerosyrans watched in silence. The sound of blade on blade or blade on buckler seemed thunderous. Soon he knew that his opponent was more than very good.

He was hurt; the back of her sword struck his left forearm hard enough to raise a lump that would resolve itself into a vivid and long-lasting bruise. She was hurt; he kicked her lower calf hard enough to save himself from her cut—and nearly hard enough to knock her down. Her shield banged him before he could take full advantage of her momentary weakness.

You'll limp tomorrow, bitch!

At the instant he had that thought she drew blood. Only great good luck saved Jarik's eyes. Her point touched his forehead, just between his wheaten brows. As he was moving backward at the time, and striking, he was little more than touched. Nevertheless the point moved in his skin, shallowly incising a backward L, so that blood flowed and he knew he would have a scar there. If he survived.

Her skill made her a good and dangerous opponent; her speed made her an incredible and deadly one; his lack of buckler was a severe handicap. Too, she seemed to fight as he did. All out, the object to destroy by any means. Even her barefoot kick made him limp a step, and hurt.

Many hands slapped many bare thighs in applause when the Kerosyrans saw the blood on his face. Then he had two-handedly struck so hard that the Black Sword sounded on her shield like a falling tree. She staggered several paces back and aside, and the Guardians again fell silent. Shralla of the sun was gone beyond the trees, and some Kerosyrans reluctantly moved aside to let the dancing yellow light of a pair of cookfires illuminate the combatants.

Are Kirrensark and those others deaf? Can't they hear this clangor of war? Are they all drunk? Perhaps drugged, he thought—*on plants or women.* And he pulled a ligament in his thigh, *willing* himself back out of reach of the drawing cut she launched at his belly. Her point whistled past the drawstring of his leggings, and she had spun and was ready before he could recover enough to swing a wild figure-8 to keep her at bay.

He was forced to do that often, in defense. He struck oftener, too, than Jilain. Blood tickled his face but did not enter his eyes. He flailed and chopped and a piece of shield jumped into the air.

He was taller. His arm was longer and his blade was longer. And he knew that he was more than good—just as she was.

He danced away from a slash, stumbled over the very

piece of shield he had chopped out, and fell backward.
Only the strength of his arm saved him from her ax-like
chop, which came down on the blade he interposed
horizontally. He also kicked, his buskined foot striking
her leg hard enough to knock her back and down. By the
time he was up, so was she. They circled, watching.

His foe was swift and good and Jarik had long since
passed from nervousness to worry. She was superlatively
supple; athletically, acrobatically fast and sinuous. She
was cat and serpent and warrior. There was strength in
her legs with their unusually developed round calves, a
dancer's legs. There was strength in her firm round arms
that showed no muscle but did not jiggle the slightest and
were not rounded with fat. Her eyes darted their hazelnut
gaze and she feinted and Jarik must dance, dodge, leap.
Her buckler was always there when he struck, a short oval
decorated with Osyran serpents in blue and green
entwined on a background that dangerously drew the eyes
and now dangerously flashed with the firelight. Her arm
flashed and her leg was a blur and her sword a bluish
streak. Jarik ducked low. He struck at her shins, saw them
leave the ground, straight up. He fell back and scrambled
away, knowing that in descending from that vertical leap
she would strike down at him, strongly. He rolled and
pawed and hurled himself to his feet and whirled in time
to strike away her sword. A constant miracle, her shield
was there to take his backstroke.

They circled. He struck a whistling blow that chopped
a wedge from her shield's edge with such force that she
staggered back. She used her sword, just, to deflect his
second chopping stroke.

The woman recovered with incredible rapidity. She
struck, and Jarik had to dodge so violently that he bowled
over an onlooking Guardian in her forties. She screamed
and while Jilain's gaze was off him for those three seconds
he got around her shield's edge and nicked her hip.

"Uh." It was her only sound. Blood ran down her leg

while she backed. Jarik followed up. With a mad sudden
unceasing flurry of blows he wearied her left arm and
chopped her shield with crash after crash. Sparks and
flinders flew, and larger pieces of the ragged buckler. It
became splinters, and now other Guardians muttered.

Jilain did not panic. Half-stooping, she hewed at
Jarik's leg. He struck away her sword and struck again so
fast that his blade was an attacking snake. Not fast
enough, still; she interposed the remnant of her buckler.
With a terrible thud and splintering sound followed by a
ringing clang, he chopped through ruined wood to the
brass boss, which his blade dented deeply. She staggered
back from that blow, and Jarik strode in, and like a
licking tongue her sword's tip opened his thigh in a
horizontal line.

He did not feel it. He did not know it. The cut had
nearly missed and was not deep. It bled. Blood was on his
arm, and his face, and now it ran down his leg as it did
hers. He swung hard and struck, half-turning with the
power behind the stroke. Flinders of shield flew from her
hand so that more than one other Guardian must duck.
At that, almost miraculously, her blade sought him. It
struck the silver bracer on his sword-arm, just missing the
elbow. The clangor was loud and the force enough to hurl
his arm aside and half-turn him. The Band of Snowmist
was not even scored, but only by kicking his opponent's
ankle hard enough to hurt his own foot did Jarik save
himself from being spitted.

He pounced backward, spun completely around to
build an irresistible momentum, and launched a stroke
vicious enough to behead a calf.

For an instant warrior's instinct started the Kerosyran
to turn partly away while lifting her shield arm. Had Jilain
completed that automatic action she'd have lost hand and
face, for such was the force of his blow to shear through
the one and chop into the other. She did not; she
remembered that her shield was gone. Desperately, with

perhaps two seconds to live, she went to one knee while
lifting her right arm, elbow pointed at him, her blade
slanted horizontally to catch his stroke.

That chopping slash was supposed to end the battle,
and it did.

Her defensive maneuver succeeded in saving her,
though the impact made her teeth clack together and
grate. Her arm gave, but not fully, for she was strong.
Strangely, the ruby on her own breast cut her own
forearm. Her iron blade, despite its thickness, could not
withstand such a terrible blow of the Black Sword of
god-metal. It snapped.

A seven-inch length of broken iron whizzed past her
head, snipping one purplish-blue lock, and only just
missed two others of Kerosyr before it was stopped by the
upflung buckler of a Guardian. Jilain stared at it. The end
of her sword, imbedded in the wood to the depth of a
finger-joint.

From one knee, Jarik's opponent stared up at him.
They stared at each other, warrior and warrior, bluejay
eyes and hazelnut. Servant of Osyr and of the Lady of
the Snowmist and the Iron Lords; enemies sweaty from
long combat; warrior and warrior, man and woman.

Jarik did not strike.

"You ... *bested* this one!"

Her gasp, her tone betold her surprise and more; awe,
perhaps. Jarik knew that this superb red feather warrior
could hardly believe she said such words, much less the
fact they admitted.

He nodded, sweaty and panting and no less impressed
than she. "Drop that piece of ruined iron, and stand."
Blood trickled from between his brows.

She did. Other Guardians honored the promise of
champion and ruler, and did not lunge at the victorious
foreigner. Jilain had gone pale, but stood and assumed a
bravely open stance to receive her death blow. Looking
into her eyes, Jarik extended the Black Sword. She held

her eyes unblinkingly open while the point approached them.

The cold metal touched her forehead, and she stood still. With care Jarik pricked her above and between her thick black brows, and he turned the Sword, just a little. Blood trickled. She made no sound and did not move. Jarik stepped back, thrust the Sword's tip into the ground to remove the spot of blood, and wiped it on his leggings to remove the earth.

"I turned the blade to make a wedge," he told her. "You will have a scar of me, as I have of you." He turned to Osyrrain. "Guardian of Guardi—" he began, and saw her dark eyes swerve to look past him. His grip on his hilt was loose, and he dropped the Sword in his desperate sideward lunge.

The dagger Jilain wielded in an overhand stab narrowly missed her ruler as the Kerosyran warrior plunged past her intended victim, Jarik Blacksword.

9

Two Scars

Jilain of Kerosyr fought as Jarik fought; blindly, madly,
without rules. She had been bested but had not owned
defeat. Her sword was ruined and the enemy had his, and
again faced her ruler. With her dagger Jilain sought to
finish him, from behind. She missed because Osyrrain's
eyes warned him and he lunged away. Osyrrain, seeing
that long blade rushing at her, screamed. Jilain's speed
and suppleness enabled her to turn the blade aside.

She recovered and half turned to face Jarik—whose
right hand sprang out to close on her right wrist.

Almost instantly she launched her other hand. Her fist
struck his chest with a meaty sound on impact with the
plate of muscle. Immediately her leg jerked up to drive her
knee into his groin. Jarik threw himself back, bending,
holding both her arms at the full extent of his. Her knee
missed him and flashed up between them. His left hand
released her wrist and rushed down. With a loud slap it
caught her thigh, whose firmness was a surprise. This
woman was one smooth-skinned mass of sinew, firm as a
serpent and nigh as sinuous.

Jarik yanked her leg upward. For the first time she
made a sound beyond "uh," though this gasp was little
more. He did not let go her dagger-hand, but let its wrist
twist and her arm wrench as she fell back with a grunt.

Hanging on, he went down with her. The dropping of

his shin onto her midsection brought a whoof from her and made her eyes bulge. Again, he felt muscle. This...Jilain had borne?

She struck left-handed and he only just got his left forearm up in time to deflect the blow from his nose. The impact of her fist on his silver bracer brought a grunt of pain from the Kerosyran.

Partially squatting, partially kneeling on her stomach so that he was safe from her legs, Jarik held her right arm. Both their arms trembled with strain. He knew surprise unto astonishment at the strength he had to exert to keep the dagger away from him. Her fist struck his chest again. With his left he struck hers, and opened his hand to slap her face. It was no gentle tap. Jilain's eyes rolled and her teeth clashed.

Using both hands, he forced the dagger from her grasp, slapped her other cheek, and set her knife at her chest. The point pressed just beside the ruby that flashed there on one hummock of flesh.

"Be still!"

She was still.

"Twice I have defeated you, best of Osyr's Guardians. Nor do I know any other man who could stand up to Jilain of Kerosyr. I had to destroy your sword to do it. I spoke you awrong; you are no girl. Give it up now."

He wondered why he had diminished his victory by making the vanquished a gift of so many words. Her teeth were clenched. She glared up at him, seemingly heedless of how her panting endangered her breast. A defeated lioness stared balefully up at him—a lion.

"Male or female, you are a fantastic fighter and nigh-matchless warrior. I've no wish to splash your blood. Acknowledge me master."

"One...wiil...not!"

Grim of mouth, Jarik studied her face. "What a woman," he breathed, and with a great sigh he released her and stood, all in one flexing of his legs. He stood over her, and his mark was on her hip, and on her forehead, as her mark was on his thigh and forehead. She continued to stare balefully up at him while he stepped back.

Seeing her eyes roll, he looked around. Jarik faced leveled spears and above them grim visages. And he faced Osyrrain.

"You are indeed a mickty warrior, Jarik Blacksword. You have defeated our best. It is a shame to . . . waste your self and your seed. Nevertheless for your violation of the temple and the Pythoness and for laying rough hands on me, you must die."

Jarik was thunderstruck. He had thought—

"That has not been settled? I spared you when I could have slain or thrust you onto her blade, and I defeated your champion—twice."

"We have no such custom or law," Osyrrain said serenely. "Flickting you was her idea, and nowt else."

"You live because I did not kill you!"

"No; one lived before you came here, and woold have lived withoot this strife had you not come."

It was the sort of serene logic Jarik was not fond of; it spoke against him, and inarguably because it *was* logic. He considered his chances. He considered fighting, and thus he thought of the Black Sword, and so it came to him, while Jilain was rising. The points of three spears touched him as his hand enwrapped his weapon's hilt. He knew he dared make no fight or try again to seize the ruler. If she ordered him slain now, he would fight. Otherwise—a chance remained. It was his bane, Jarik mused cheerlessly. He had fought, and won, and in the doing of it he had accomplished nothing. He had only spent some energy and a little blood.

A voice cut the silence, and he recognized it; the Moon-Mother spoke.

"The sun is gone," she said. "The moon rules. He must not be slain until the sun again rules."

Osyrrain scowled and swiftly composed her face into an expression of apparent serene agreement. Slowly, that none might mistake his movements for warlike ones, he reversed the Sword. He extended it hilt first—past Osyrrain.

"You are like no other woman. I think you have met the only man who could defeat you. Hold this."

After a moment of looking at the extended hilt and at his eyes, Jilain took the weapon that had destroyed hers. Her face bore no happy look. She looked profoundly thoughtful.

Ershain bound Jarik's wrists behind him as Osyrrain directed. Ershain's features bore no happy look. Jilain stared at his face. The firelight made her face look gaunt, and emphasized the high cheekbones. A similar shadowed hollow showed at each inner hip, where she was padded only with sinew. The lines of her stomach were as narrow as Jarik's hand which, laid flat, could have covered that little belly. For the first time he noted that her short, sweat-wet hair parted on the right to reveal a great deal of forehead. Her eyes stared as if she were deeply troubled. She held the Black Sword with its tip just touching the ground before her. She had done nothing about the trickle of blood that had run down to harden under her left eye, and he remembered that his face, too, bore coagulated blood. Her forehead was marred by it, low and almost between her brows, as he knew his was.

Osyrrain went around her dais and again mounted it from behind. She did not seat herself.

"He who has violated the temple and the Pythoness, slain the Serpent of Osyr and handled Osyrrain, must die by the lickt of day. He will be held, bound, in the doe-hut, to die at sun's zenit' on the morrow."

While Kirrensark and the others enjoy strong drink and women all night I will lie bound, Jarik thought. *Kirrensark, Kirrensark my ancient enemy—I have never slain you and now I enable you and your Hawkers to dally drunkenly! But I'll not precede you by much, in death. Surely these madwomen—once they are sure of being with child—slay the fathers just as later they slay the sons!*

He let his glance swerve to Jilain.

Holding the Black Sword idly, she was gazing at him. A frown set wrinkles to her smooth high forehead— smooth save for the wound he had so carefully, so arrogantly put on it. Thoughtful she was; troubled perhaps, puzzled, perhaps. *It does not matter*, Jarik thought, and he looked back at Osyrrain.

"What you do is evil, Osyrrain."

"What we do was commanded longer than long ago, by the god, and for the god."

With the assistance of the hand of the Moon-Mother, she stepped from the dais. She turned, and Jarik looked without pleasure on the bare hindcheeks of a ruler. In a swirl of cloak and furs the Moon-Mother stepped around her and preceded her into the great house. *The cloak of some man they used and murdered,* Jarik thought, watching two Guardians follow close.

He stared after them until Ershain's hand tugged at his bound wrists.

"The doe house," he muttered, and with a stiff short motion, he bowed his head to Jilain.

"Come," Ershain said, and Jarik went. He was aware of the gazes of many eyes, all brown, and among them Jilain's.

10

Out of the Body!

"Grey and white color do not belong to the same thing at
the same time; ergo their components are opposed."
"A false argument depends on the first statement in it."
—Aristotle

"So far as man is concerned, evolution has been merely a
zigzag process up from protoplasm to ectoplasm."
—Edward S. Van Zile

It is possible to tie hands behind the back so that the
person bound is not uncomfortable. The forearms
pressed together, palms at elbows, the bindings just tight
enough, and not too tight...

This the Guardians had not done. Jarik's wrists were
crossed and the cord wound thrice about them, then
drawn up between to tighten the linkage and bind each
wrist individually. Very simple. He would not be
escaping. Not alone; not without help. Nor was it
comfortable. He was walked into the good-sized hut and
left to himself. Ershain left him standing in the
windowless, unlit interior. He stood a long while.
Darkness gradually faded to dimness as his pupils
enlarged. Arms and legs twitched, from the tension of a
long combat in which he'd had to concentrate and strive
with all skill.

A woman!

He shook his head at that. And she had almost . . . ! He walked about. Always there was consciousness of his bound arms. Of a small, growing strain to his shoulders. To those human wings called shoulder blades. He felt no gratitude that his captors had not given him the real stressful straining pain of bound elbows. After a long while of standing and walking, he went to the door. Two guards lounged just outside. They were ready for him, both young and lean white feather Guardians. He withdrew, and paced a bit more.

At last, arms secured behind him, he went carefully down—calves tightening and toes trying to clench, to clutch—into a squat. In constant teetering danger of falling backward, without arms for balance. On his haunches, legs bent double, trembly, he let himself drop back. He expected the jar of impact on sitting, and made no sound when his buttocks thumped onto hard earth. He sat.

By now he was able to see. He looked about him to discover that he had been stupid. The doe hut was furnished with a pallet; fabric and husks and fur. Pox and plague! All he'd had to do was walk over to that dark corner and sit on the pallet!

Now . . . rather than perform the ridiculous calisthenics of getting himself to his feet with his arms immobilized behind him, Jarik scooted to the pallet, backward. Sitting, knees up. Push with the legs, scoot back, draw up the legs, push again. Moving backward like a crippled grasshopper. At the pallet, he sort of lunge-wallowed onto it. Otherwise he'd only have folded and bunched it up under him.

He sat there a long while, a long long while, assuring himself that there was no escape. He just could not free his hands. Nor was there anything in the hut to use in trying to saw the cords. Outside, he heard the sounds of a village shading into night-quiet. A village of females only. (Kirrensark and the others disporting themselves with women, turning white feathers into red . . .) He strained against the cords now and then, because he was human, and male, and Jarik, and had to try now and then, straining. Damn the others! *He* had to be the hero! Yet come the morrow they'd all die, just the same. They, however, were not bound. They were not alone, the others off *Seadancer*.

His straining accomplished nothing save to assure him that there was no escape, and that slim cords, cutting into wrist-flesh, *hurt*. Thinking of his companions, also, hurt.

It was dark in the hut and he heard the sounds of a village of women growing sleepy, all without listening to them and their sounds.

To die tomorrow!

Iron Lords! Destruction, and Annihilation, and Dread! Where are you! Help me! (He could not remember their strange *real* names, which were long, and strange.) *Snowmist!* Help me! I am to die tomorrow. On your service! I don't want to die on the morrow—I don't *deserve* to die on the morrow! Help me. Free me!

Gods, he found, did not respond to mental pleas, whether they heard or no, across leagues and leagues of ocean. And Jarik was too ridiculously, boyishly proud to call out aloud, or even murmur. The guards, the Guardian guards, might hear and snicker or call in a taunt. Jarik could not bear that. Better to remain silent and seem stoic. Thus Jarik, poor Jarik who wanted and needed to be and Be.

It was not fair. Nothing had ever been fair, that the weavers wove for him.

He had been a good boy, and all his people had been annihilated, extirpated, destroyed. (And Dread, don't forget dread Dread!) Stath had goaded him, and insulted Torsy, and at last Jarik had fought him sword against sword and killed him—and been exiled, for Stath was the firstman's son, of Ishparshule-wark. As Oak he had saved that trapper and got them accepted into Blackiron—and been nothing there, nothing, for he had not been able to heal and they'd had no need of a man of weapons. Until those three hawkers had raped and murdered Torsy and Nevre and Jarik had gone and got the Black Sword and slain those men. And *because* he had the Black Sword, the Iron Lords had not known that the other hawkers were attacking Blackiron and killing villagers. Seeking vengeance all his life, living only for vengeance or so he told himself, driven; he had been suffered by the Iron Lords to keep the Sword, and given mail and a commission by the Iron Lords, and transported by the Iron Lords across the impassable mountains. At once he had seen a man being attacked by three, and had rushed down and saved him. And that man turned out to be he on whom Jarik had sought vengeance since he was eight years old; since That Day. He had sought to kill Snowmist, for the Iron Lords, and had instead become her slave. He had freed the Pythoness, surely a noble and heroic act, and because of that act she was slain and he condemned. He had met the queen's champion in fair combat, and been shocked; he had to fight long and hard! Yet he had won. And then over her again—*her*! A woman—and what had it availed him?

Naught. Here he sat, bound. To die on the morrow. It was not fair.

He did that at which he had much practice: Jarik pitied himself, and wallowed in that self-pity.

It isn't fair, Jarik thought with bitterness, and came to the bitter understanding that others had, and would—few others. "Fair" was for children. Real living was not a game, with rules. "Fair" was not a part of it. "Fair" was not a part of the plan for people, the plan of the world, of the universe. The weavers wove, and they were blind. "Fair" was an invention of humankind, and humankind did not make the rules. The gods did. The gods made the warp and woof, and the weavers wove the fabric of the life of each woman and man.

His brain had made an enormous breakthrough, though he did not know it. He would merely not expect fairness again. In that was acceptance and a form of happiness ... or "happiness."

His arms hurt. That is, his bound wrists and shoulderblades were not comfortable, and his shoulders were beginning to cramp, to hurt. No matter; tomorrow they were going to kill him. Because he was Jarik. Because he had freed the Pythoness (to die). Because he had served the Lady of the Snowmist. Because he had tried to serve the Iron Lords.

Death. Die die die death. Not fair. Death.

Hailstones and pox and plague on the Iron Lords! Worse on the Lady of the Snowmist; the freezing-death of winter on her!

Thus in his miserable mind did Jarik damn them, Jarik who was damned.

He was Jarik; he thought about killing ...

Condemned, he condemned living gods, not his condemnor. Osyrrain. Or her champion: Jilain. Marvelous woman! Filthy rotten mange-ridden bitch ... fantastic warrior and marvelous woman!

Ugly wench! (No she wasn't.)

I ... want her. I ... respect her more than anyone I've ever seen! Anyone. She is good! She nearly bested me—and when I bested her, she was not bested at all, but fought on. And almost stabbed me from behind!

He was very glad, at least, that he had marked her forehead with the scarring wound she had put on his. He was very glad at least that he had put defeat on that superb warrior and excellent opponent. What a fighter! Yet she was not huge of arm, and little muscle showed on her. If justice existed, if fairness did, he'd be free now, for he had defeated the best warrior he had ever faced. (How could a woman possibly ... well, no use thinking about that! She had, nearly. She was.) To have defeated her was more than to have slain Stath, or those three who had raped and slain Torsy and Nevre who might have been his woman, or even the two who had sought to have Torsy that day on the beach.

What use to try to call the Black Sword to him now? If someone now held it, it would not come. If it were not held, it would be seen, so eerily traveling here to its owner—*owner*! He knew elation at that thought, until he remembered that on the morrow he died—and they would follow it in and take it and hold it and that would be that. Better he did not try to call it to him.

That woman! That incredible warrior.

Girl, he had called her! Plague and hail, she had probably ceased being a *girl* at about age eight, when he had ceased being a boy. (Or would be partly a girl all her life, as he would be partly a boy, seeking, striving, seeking...)

He was thinking about that incredible woman when, uncomfortable, bound, in some pain, he accomplished the incredible. A weary Jarik Blacksword fell asleep.

He did not know that he had. He thought that he was awake, and that the Lady of the Snowmist came to him. (Or perhaps that was so.) She came, all in white and silver and grey, a vision passing beautiful. A frosty, sparkling silver mask was part of her helm and covered her features, covered her head, and it was like snow at dawning after a night of freezing rain, all sparkly and bright and fulgurant. Snowmist. No eyeslits pierced her mask, though high-arched "brows" of darker grey provided an expression of hauteur. Masked and without eyes, he seemed to stare regally. The "mouth" was shaped, rather than slitted like those in the masks worn by the Iron Lords. It was, somehow, a lovely female mouth. Part of the mask. As the mask was part of the helmet, attached to the shaped, close-fitting silver helm that formed a short dome. It was winged. The wings were white. The hilt of her sheathed sword was polished silver and its pommel a strange stone that was without color and yet, faceted, it glinted with many colors at her slightest movement. Over the silver-grey armor on each of her wrists, there gleamed silver bracers that were identical to Jarik's. The pearl-grey gloves that sheathed her hands flashed and scintillated, seemingly dusted with silver shavings.

Such was the Lady of the Snowmist. So were the gods formed and accoutred and masked. No part of them showed, neither skin nor eye.

And her voice was liquid silver floating down a mountain stream:

"Fairness does exist. The wrong use of a thing is far worse than the non-use, and the contrary of an evil is sometimes a good—and sometimes an evil."

Jarik dared say, "But then grey and white color can belong to the same thing at the same time?"

"It is self-evident. I am proof. *You* are proof, Jarik."

"You have said that it cannot!"

"That is not possible. How can anything untruthful be said?"

Jarik shook his head desperately. "A force of purest white," he said slowly, groping for words and thoughts to back words. "That is the way you see yourself. A force for good only. 'To protect and rescue human rights.' Yet . . . to manipulate, to kidnap, to drive men to war on others—and women—to murder, to lie . . . with or without legal authority . . ."

"We have legal authority, Jarik, poor Jarik," he was told, and before him stood one of the Iron Lords, or perhaps all three: Destruction, and Annihilation, and Dread. "We *are* the law. None else exists, save the natural one which is survival of the most fortunate, or strongest. How ugly! How unworthy! We are the law. There is then no way that we can act illegally! Even you can see that, Jarik. That is logic. That is not semantics; We are a legally constituted authority, above all others. We do not require approval, or seek or need it. We have no time to consider individuals, even masses. We must look at all the history that is to be, that can be. We cannot pause; cannot afford to consider 'fairness' and 'rights' and individual sensibilities!"

Confused, Jarik was bold: "In other words, you do just what you want, for no one has any control over you."

"We love the concept of humankind too much to do otherwise. We must try, as we always have, to save humankind; to create order, no matter what the measures necessary—or the consequences."

"Murder?" Doomed, Jarik was bold.

"We deny murder. We do deny. We do order assassination, but to save humankind, not ourselves."

"Then the motive justifies the crime?"

"Crime? We are the authority."

Jarik tried again: "Then the motive justifies the act?"

"Does a noble goal justify the means employed to reach it?"

"You ask me, a human? Assassination is only a pretty word, invented to cover a specific type of murder and make it sound as less than murder."

"Murder is only an ugly word, invented to describe a specific type of death! Shall we invent still another word to describe the death of a god?"

"The killing of a god is murder the same as—" Jarik broke off. He realized that a door had been opened invitingly to him, that he had entered a room that was a trap, and that he himself had kicked the argument's door shut behind him. He had slain, and he had sought to slay a god. If slaying was murder, then . . . "Slaying can be justified," he said slowly. "It justifies itself, when the reason is self-defense or the motive is for the good."

Laughter swirled about him like ribbons tied at one end only and left to the wind. The ship listed slowly and sank. Of its armored crew and passengers, few swam safely to shore. Those who did were promptly slain. *I will slay her*, Jarik said.

"'Assassination' then, Jarik."

"Assassination is only a pretty word," he heard himself say, and could not prevent it while he knew he spoke both to the Iron Lords and Lady Snowmist, "invented to cover a specific type of murder and make it sound less than murder. The slain was important: a lord, a god, not just anyone. So he was 'assassinated', rather than just slain, murdered, like anyone else, like lesser people."

"If a man should make exception and contend that his

statements and opinions are capable of admitting contrary qualities, his contention is unsound."

The universe rocked but Jarik persisted despite having heard logic. "No matter what the god, the goal, the accomplishment, murder is not good behavior. It is evil. Not white, but black. Grey is white with black mixed into it, and black is stronger."

"If that is so," his answer came; "if evil is more powerful than good; if chaos is more powerful than order; then we are all lost, Jarik. Gods and humans alike. Where the new faith is involved, there are seldom simple motives. The new faith is humankind, Jarik, and simple motives will always be hard to come by, save for simple people. So black is stronger. So white cannot continue to exist when black is added, in however minute a quantity. For the result is grey. Thus grey exists and thus black and white and grey *can* be mixed and exist simultaneously! Very well. You, and we, then, are naturally congruent organisms. It is not true to say that everything that may be good or bad must be either good or bad. There are intermediate hues between the contrarieties of black and white."

Help!

After the sweeping, the broom straws were meticulously collected. Jarik was staggering, in brain and body. Yet it was one more in the series of shocks that was beginning to make less and less impression on him; shock was becoming commonplace. Suddenly there was no more voice. Suddenly there was no more dust and no more boulders and no more road.

He fell.

He fell for minute after minute, shrieking and writhing as his wide eyes reported the kaliedoscopic agony of sky - ground - horizon - ground - sky - forest - sky - ground - ground-ground-GROUND his guts floating his mouth streaming vomit that splashed over him as he fell, screaming with the sky blasting his eyes yet fading, fading, moving ever farther away with terror mounting screaming and the ground ground GROUND rushing up and rushing up closer and closer to receive his pinwheeling, breathless, vomiting body with its floating organs until with the impact it would explode to send blood and internal organs and bones and muscle tearing, ripping, exploding squishing out through the flesh and it went on and on for minutes and more minutes with the ground rushing up and getting closer and closer and closer and closer until he was going to IMPA.

We should judge only by those things 'good' or 'bad' that are within our power, Jarik. If an external thing gives you pain, it is not this thing that causes your pain, but your own judgment of it.

Guide?

Awake, Jarik, you are not dead.

That does not make me happy, Guide.

Nor did that coming to puberty that was on you when I visited you before, Jarik, (unintelligible) *Jarik. It is not life or living that makes you unhappy, Jarik, but you. It is not the thing that gives you pain, but your own judgment of it. And he who says that black and white cannot simultaneously exist in the same receptacle is a fool, Jarik-who-is-Two-Men.*

You said—you said that I am a twoness that must be a oneness . . . and that that can come about only by my taking on a third part, that will unify me into one.

And you said that you did not understand, and I told you, my son, my poor Jarik, that it would be agony to you that you did not understand. And hasn't it been so! Even so, the agony will continue when you are whole—three as one—although it will be a different sort of agony, Jarik, and you will know happiness. Some happiness. A part of you is a tree, and a part of you is a woman, and two parts of you lie on an island, close to union.

Jarik felt neither hurt nor heat nor cold nor the stir of air nor aught that his body touched and so he knew that he had separated from his body as he had done that other time—those other times. And the Guide was there, his

Guide who had come to him that night of his reaching puberty. Tall and slender, with aristocracy in his face and legs and arms well molded. He was of no color that Jarik could describe, or would remember, this man, this god, who was his Guide. A slim, plaited beard covered and depended from his chin only, so that his well-cut face was hairless and smooth. He bore in one hand a sword, long and black and shining, while in the other he held a staff. It was the length of the sword, but with a crook at one end, and white. The Guide was naked, and his genitals were huge.

Jarik remembered that other time.

Please—please do not make me look again at colliding worlds whence came the gods, Jarik pleaded. *It is agony, and horror. It hurts.*

The Guide spoke, and yet his lips did not move. He was as a statue. The words formed themselves in Jarik's mind. (*As they must,* Jarik thought; *without my body, I have no ears to hear! My body is in the doe hut—and this time I don't know whether I want to return to it or not! It is to die on the morrow, my body!*)

And he heard the Guide: *This time I shall show you nothing,* (something)-*son Jarik. This time I am come to tell you something; to tell you what you are, and of what. Attend, and put to use that good mind you have been given, Jarik who is Two Men . . . soon to be Three Who Is One!*

And Jarik gave listen, though he had no body and thus no ears.

"Jarik . . . once there was nothing. Nothing. Consider: there was no one and no thing. Then, there was a crash as of a million million thunders—or was there, with no one to hear? And the light as of a million million bolts of lightning, though no one saw it. Out of that cataclysm and chaos came incandescent gasses in vast boiling roiling clouds in many colors—or was there color, with no one to see? Some gasses joined, and others, and others. And through a million million lifetimes though there was no one living, matter was born of gas. Matter: that which composes things, Jarik. Looms, and hoes, and swords, and trees, and planets. From that were universes born. From universes were suns born; vast floating self-contained pools of incandescent gasses a million million times hotter than hot. The suns drew, and pulled. The matter was gathered into the suns, and returned to gas; to flame. Some little of it was not. Instead it chose to become minions of the suns. To spin about them forever, like the outbuildings of warks, like the people of warks around their leader, the firstman.

"They were hot, hot; a million times hotter than hot. Plow-wood and sword-metal were molten and could not harden to make *things*, even creatures. And thus passed a million million million lifetimes, with no one living them. And the universes established an order. Each sun was part of it, and established its own order. Your sun did, which was my sun. Each world became a part of that order, and its moons. Or moon. Your world did, Jarik with its one moon. They cooled. It cooled. Matter was born and became solid. Molecules became vapor and vapor cooled to become water. Oceans and mountains, and then land and eventually soil and grass and trees aspiring toward the sun, and creatures, simple creatures in the seas: the simplest of creatures. And they became more complex; and one or a dozen crawled forth, ugly and slimy but aspiring toward the sun. One survived, out of the sea, and from it came land creatures, half sea creature, and from them too came land creatures that were *of the land, for* the land, and they grew and developed while a million million lifetimes passed while trees grew and the sun ruled in its glorious warming blaze. And a squatty hairy hideous toothy hand-footed little beast picked up a stick fallen from a tree. With it he beat off another, and used a sharp-ended stick to spear a fish for his belly, and sharpened a stick to spear an enemy animal whose teeth and claws and muscles were better. And it grew, Jarik, and grew, and lifetimes passed and it became Jarik."

All these words the Guide said into Jarik's mind. There

was silence then, while the Guide said naught and Jarik's head swam, and the weavers wove.

The Guide said, *Do you understand that, Jarik*?

Jarik was horribly honest: "No."

The voice of the Guide came strong and harsh then, and sharp with anger.

"Then once there was a Great Man, and he was alone and he wanted company, for all around him there was nothing. So he created the earth, and set it to spinning, with trees and mountains and seas on it. Since it was shrouded in the darkness He had decided to dispel, He created the sun, for light and warmth, and He set it in the sky. And He set the moon, too, for light at night, and surrounded it with the myriad stars like gemstones to draw the eyes of men upward toward Him. Then he created people. A man. A woo-man. He told them to populate His world ... and they did, and did, and grew, and lifetimes passed and they became Jarik. Do you understand that, Jarik?"

With happiness and pride Jarik practically shouted it: "Yes!"

The Guide's sigh was cosmic and cosmological. "Very well, Jarik. Very well. You are intelligent, and a fit model of your kind. You have just doomed your kind, on this world, to religion."

Jarik did not know what that word was and he knew that the Guide was displeased. He knew too that there was nothing he could do about it, for he did not know what had happened, or what he had done, or what was meant.

"Accept the emotional refuge then, Jarik: believe in gods. Accept me, for I am God! Religion *is* genetic then; it must be, as imagination and stupidity are, just as (incomprehensible) maintained. You must subordinate yourself to charisma and sacralization—and doubtless, in time, to dogma. For now your kind has only gods, and myths; soon you will have religion. What a soaring vapid capacity for hypocrisy and self-deception we more-than-animals have!

"Subordinate yourself, even your very welfare, to the

good or 'good' of the tribe, the society—the tribe of humankind—and try to find pleasure in that, as ants and bees do. Yet it will aid the development of your kind, and its spread, even while it hinders it. White cannot continue to exist when black is added, even in minute quantity. Deceive yourselves and each other in behavior directed to the group, and for...gods. By it you will survive...in Ignorance!"

"Good exists," Jarik said. "Gods exist," he said, as hopeful as he was dogged.

"Of course. It just has not occurred to your squalid kind to *worship* them, to set themselves up as sole interpreters for the gods. It will. You have doomed your kind, and this world, to religion."

"What is r—"

"Wake up, Jarik."

"What is rel—"

"*Wake up*, Jarik!"

Jarik awoke, with his brain spinning and staggering and his arms assailed as by a thousand stinging ants, for he lay on them in the doe hue of the wark of the Guardians. He became aware of a hand on him, of hands, of another body touching his. Someone squatted there, in the darkness of the doe hut that was his prison. Someone spoke—again:

"Jarik?" The voice came in a whisper. "Wake up, Jarik, and be quiet."

A bit of moonlight was sneaking in at the doorway, and by it he saw the faint glint of metal. A dagger. She held it, naked and close to his bound body. She was not the Guide, nor yet the Lady of the Snowmist, but the woman he had defeated, Jilain.

11

Jilain Kerosyris

Still in dreams it comes upon me that I once on wings did
   soar;
But or e'er my flight commences this my dream must all be
   o'er.

—From the Persian

"You were dreaming."

He was not sure that he had been. Had he dreamed, or
left his body behind to travel—elsewhere? Yet he was not
sure that he was not dreaming now. His mind was a
vaporous swirl of confusion. Jarik strove to blink and
force himself back to reality. If this was reality, he was
bound in the doe hut, with Jilain squatting beside him,
wearing next to nothing and telling him that he had been
dreaming.

"Yes," he said, in little more than a grunt, and he felt
very good about having gotten out that much. His head
remained full of words and visions, of chaos and
beginnings. Of good and bad gods and Guide.

"You are no happy woman," she said.

That was no less disconcerting. "What?"

"This one said that you are no happy—oh. Man, man!
Girl and boy; woman and man," she recited, reminding
herself. "Jarik: man. Jarik who dreams, Jarik who is the
best warrior anywhere . . . why is he no happy man?"

He swallowed, and the act gave him considerable discomfort and pain. That rapidly translated into a seething, for he was Jarik and could not weaken himself by admitting his misery; could not demean himself by admitting his weakness. It was hard, being Jarik.

"I am bound, and you have your dagger in your hand," he said low, almost snarling. A helpless animal, braced for death, telling itself that it was resigned. "Use it. My happiness or unhappiness is mine. Just use the dagger—but never forget that I won." And Jarik, because he was Jarik, added, "Twice."

"Use it? In a moment. This one is not happy either. And—"

"Should I pretend to care? *You* are not to die on the morrow!"

"And oh yes, Jarik," she said as though he had not spoken, "This one knows you defeated her." After a moment she added, "Twice."

"Your happiness cannot concern me," he told himself. "Use the dagger."

"Learn patience, Jarik Blacksword. Answer this. You came here only for the Rod of Osyr?"

He blinked. Rolled his eyes in the darkness. What had this to do with...

Impatiently, impatient to get death done with, now that the Dark Brother was here for him in the form of a dagger in a woman's hand, he replied as if angrily. "Yes."

"Nothing else," she pressed in that strangely soft voice that might have belonged to a dove.

"Can we stop this silly chatter? I was *sent* here for the Rod of Osyr. Yes. Else I'd never have come to this manless middenheap."

"Know you that Osyr is god, and the wand is his, and all Guardians exist only for Him ... and this one is Osyr's champion?"

"Yes, I know all that," he said quietly, angrily into darkness. His shoulders ached. His fingers tingled and his whipped back was stiffening. "*I* defeated Osyr's serpent, *and* his Pythoness, *and* his champion."

"Aye. You have fairly won the Rod. Wit' it, you will leave Kerosyr? You are content with the White Rod of our god?"

Could she mean— A flood of blood cascaded from every vein in Jarik's head to pool in his stomach. He was left chilly and prickly hot at once. Was it possible that she intended to let him go?

He said, "Aye."

Deftly and swiftly she used the dagger to cut him loose. He chewed into his lip as, slowly, he brought his hands around his body. The return of circulation, coupled with the flexing of long-straitened muscles, was *pain.*

"Here is the White Rod. The wand of Osyr, and I am traitor. Go."

He looked at it in the darkness. The White Wand. She had brought it to him, and freed him. *You have fairly won the Rod,* she said. Fairly! "Fair" and the concept of fairness . . . had it been a dream? If so, why had that come upon him this night, here, where this female warrior he had defeated seemed bound by her code of fairness, as she and her people were bound by the promises they made—all without using the personal pronoun? Kerosyr; where promises took precedence over ego. And "fairness" over loyalty or duty?

Jarik looked at her, or tried to in the dimness of the doe hut. Warrior or no, he was aware of her nearness and radiant warmth. He was aware of her as the woman she was. And of himself as male. He did not like that. He realized that he could not be false with her. Jarik did not like that, either.

Kirrensark was his enemy and Jarik had saved his life and sailed with him. Jilain was his enemy and she freed him. Were enemies not enemies? What then of the Iron Lords, whom he had tried to serve until *she* forced him into her service? And what of Her? The Lady of the Snowmist?

When I return, if I return, he told himself, *she will answer questions for me. She must!*

To Jilain Kerosyris, enemy become friend, he said all in

darkness, "I cannot go without those who came with me. The other men."

"All . . . all of them are drunkenly asleep. Sated, with drink and women. Please go. One's sisters must not be slain. Do you realize what this one has *done*?"

He said nothing. He did not want her thinking that way, lest she change her mind. Yes, he knew what she had done, and was doing. He pondered. Would she do more? Would she believe him?

"They need not be slain," he said earnestly. "None need be slain, Jilain. Those men are my . . . my friends." They were not. "They are my fellow warriors." In a way; only in a way. Would Delath have freed him thus?

"Oh." Her reaction indicated that he had made clear explanation and that she understood and accepted.

"You are serious about freeing me, Jilain. About giving me the White Rod—about letting me go." He did not let his voice form questions.

"You won it, warrior. Yes."

He started to touch her in the hut's darkness, and he did not. For good reason he wanted to touch her; for another reason he did not. "You believe me? Trust me?"

"How can one not believe you? How can one not trust you? You have acted more honorably than the Osyrrain, and much trouble and doubt is in this one's mind because of that. You acted with more mercy, too."

Jarik was near to overwhelmed by the simple, straightforward statements. He swallowed before he spoke, intently, with his face close to hers. His mouth close to hers. Aware of her radiant warmth. "Take me to her. To Osyrrain. I shall not kill her, Jilain, nor will I harm her. There is only one way I can leave here, and that is with the others. One man cannot sail a ship, or two or three. The only way we can reach the ship is with Osyrrain as hostage. That way we can avoid combat and bloodshed. The Guardians will have to let us go, then, and I will not have to harm Osyrrain."

"Have to?"

He knew that she was considering. He remained silent, until at last he said, "You know exactly what I mean, Jilain Kerosyris."

It was all he said, and he stared into her eyes, which he could only just see. A dark glitter in the pallid haze of moonlight admitted by the hut's open door.

After a long while she spoke. "You must promise not to take her with you."

"I had not considered it. I promise. We have no desire to carry off your ruler." And he added, seeking to convince, "This one promises, warrior."

"You must promise not to harm any Guardian."

"I cannot. None will be harmed if we are not attacked. But if one tries to harm one of us, or to free Osyrrain before we are safe and ready to release her... this one cannot make that promise, Jilain."

"One believes you because you said that, Jarik. It is what you mean by 'necessary' and is understandable. It will not be *necessary* that you harm Osyrrain, Jarik Blacksword, or any Guardian. Osyrrain rules; this one commands."

"I know what you want me to promise, Jilain Kerosyris. And you know what I can promise."

"Aye." She stood, and he saw that she wore his weapons belt, sheaths in place. "Rise quietly. Move your arms. Your back will be sore. You have your circulation?"

"I have it." He had been working and working fingers full of needles. Each needle was a capillary, bringing back his blood. He rose, with the ease of recovery of resilient youth. "I have it. I am hale, warrior."

After another long silence, "Come, warrior." The voice of a dove, had this deadly warrior for Osyr, soft and pleasant. One more of his life full of paradoxes.

They shuffled for a moment, and she said, "It is as prisoner you must go, Jarik Blacksword. If you will put back your hands, one will not tie them. They will appear to be bound, and you will precede one."

Showing her his back and presenting his hands for new

bondage was the last thing Jarik wanted to do. Yet it was
she who was showing the enormous trust. He had been
honest with her because he felt it incumbent on him; she
was surely totally honest. Even so, he was Jarik, and as he
turned he was thinking that if he felt her actually begin to
bind his wrists, he would whirl and strike her very hard.
He put back his hands.

She wrapped the cord twice around each wrist, and tied
a bow-knot in one end of the cord, linking it to nothing
save itself. He was not bound.

"One will walk behind you wit' dagger in hand. We go
into the Osyrrain-house."

"Where is the Black Sword?"

"It is strange. The Moon-Mother asked for it."

"The Moon—! And does she have it?"

"Even the Osyrrain does the bidding of the Moon-
Mother."

Jarik assimilated, nodded, started forward. When he
reached the doorway she stepped beside him, with a hand
on his elbow. She spoke to someone outside.

"We emerge," she said. "This one takes the prisoner to
the Osyrrain."

"Oh. He is to die tomorrow—What does she want with
him now?"

"Perhaps you would care to ask her, Serain. She is in
no good mood. This one did not care to question her
desire—and command."

"Yes, yes, Jilain," that small voice said, "very well. You
are always right, Jilain. One wishes she were always right,
and certain, as Jilain is."

"One is busy and overlooks your tone, Serain. Come,
man."

Jarik emerged into moonlit dark, and did not glance at
Serain. He never knew what she looked like. She said
nothing more, and Jarik paced across one edge of the
walled wark to the greathouse. He glanced at the tall
slender statue of the God, and at the fur-covered throne of
the Osyrrain. A tired-looking Guardian leaned against

the building's outer wall, beside the doorway.

"Decided she wanted this big strong one after all, did she, Jil?"

"Aye. Let no one else in tonight, will you?"

"All right. Have a nice time, Sun-hair."

Jarik was bold, tired of being silent: "Better if you joined us, Guardian. I do like the way you look."

"This one has tried it, *man*. This one prefers women."

Mildly shocked in his provincialism, Jarik spoke only after he was through the doorway: "So do I."

"Leftward," Jilain's voice said behind him, and a moment later her squeezing grip on his arm surprised him. "And be silent! Remember that you were not *really* sent for. Wake her now and we are in great trouble."

We, she said. Jarik nodded. He formed an apology in his mind, and did not say it. They were not in a room. It was a passage not wide and lit only by an oil lamp burning on a semicircle of table pressed against one wall. Jarik had seen only one corridor before in all his life; in the keep of the Lady of the Snowmist. He had no name for a room that was not a room but a closed passage between rooms. He paced silently along it, and saw both their shadows once they had passed the lamp. How big he was; how small she appeared now, this woman who had come so close to defeating him with weapons!

She was neither small nor large, in truth. In truth, Jilain was shaped most emphatically like a woman.

No one else had to be met, or harmed, or lied to. Guards were not needed, within the house of the Osyrrain of the Guardians of Osyr on Kerosyr.

As shadows the two moved along the corridor of this large building that was like the temple and unlike it. He came to a door and Jilain's hand came onto his shoulder. Jarik halted. She stepped close, to murmur in his ear. She was too close; he felt against him a bare part of her he'd rather not have felt or thought about. The ruby was chill. Pressing it against him did not seem to hurt her.

"Her door," Jilain murmured. "A small lamp is kept

burning within. She may have a companion. Either you will handle that, or you will not. This one will not enter the Osyrrain's quarters as an invader."

Jarik heard her swallow, knew she felt a qualm, and feared that she might change her mind. Working at being unobtrusive, he began to slip his hands out of his simulated bonds. He discovered that to be not the work of an instant; though she had not tied the leather cord's ends together, she had wrapped it twice about each wrist. He could not merely flip it off or slip free. Clever Jilain! He had been tested, he realized. Had he made a sudden attempt to break free and turn on her, thus proving himself unworthy of trust, he'd have been—prey. He had been tested. Jarik was glad that he had passed.

"This one is trusting you, warrior. Do not harm the Osyrrain."

"Warrior: I will not."

He brought his hands around, and he had the cord that had bound him. She handed him more: two lengthy strips of supple leather no broader than his little finger. He noted that she wore the bushy tail of a squirrel over her loins. She handed him a dagger. It was his own.

He stared into her eyes for a time, holding the knife. He was aware of her hand and her nearness and her nakedness. He was aware of her. He was also aware that she wore a sword. Jarik would not ask for it. In fact—

He returned the dagger, meeting her eyes. Without breaking that locked gaze, she sheathed it. Both of them understood. The two gestures, her giving it him and his returning it, had said all that could be said between them. And he wanted to reach for her.

He did not. "Would that your name were not Jilain, but Jilye; Jilyish," he said, and turned to enter the queen's chamber while Jilain wondered what he meant.

12

Jarik Blacksword

"If so many contrary emotions can be brought so intimately into relationship...the implication is that the grievousness and the resignation, the harshness and the compassion, belong to one another."

—R. Donington

The room he entered was dark, though not black. The chamber was peculiarly *within* the building; there was no outside wall and thus no window. Jarik could see because he had been long in darkness and more recently dimness. Here it was dimmer still than out in the passage. The oil lamp was most unusual, a globe flattened on the bottom, with holes to let out a little light. He waited a few moments, standing stock-still, to be sure his eyes were adjusted to this room.

Then he was marveling, in some amusement; the queen ruled naked—and slept clothed! Her sleeping gown was long, thin, fine. It was crumpled at her loins and on one leg so that it was bare from toe to knee. Jarik wondered what her knee looked like—and smiled, remembering that he had seen it and its mate, and paid no mind!

Mindful of his feet, he went to the sleeping Osyrrain. On a little table beside her elevated bed lay a slim, single-edged eating dagger. Jarik touched its point, and left it there. Beside it lay the tail of a fox. He smiled.

He passed a loop of cord over the Osyrrain's forearm and snubbed it into a noose to hold that wrist. In a moment he had the cord around her other wrist. She awoke only as he finished the swift simple task of linking her arms behind her. Swiftly he snatched up the lovely sleek soft fluffy fox-tail: he stuffed it into Osyrrain's mouth just as she opened it to shout. He tied the furry gag in place.

She thrashed, and he had never seen such sharply prominent hipbones. Deliberately Jarik seized her in an intimate place and squeezed to hurt. She became still.

She lay moveless, thin and warm and trembling, while Jarik made sure her wrists were well bound and irremediably linked. He tied her ankles. Left her while he prowled her chamber. There was no one else. There was another door, which he opened. With a creak and a rustle and gasp, a young attendant sat bolt upright on her pallet of rushes and cloth. Jarik strode to her and seized her upper arm strongly while he set her mistress's dagger at her throat so that she could feel the edge.

"Move or make a sound and you will never know whether you roused anyone or not," he told her, and she froze.

Soon she too was gagged and secured and then gagged again; her mouth first stuffed and then bound around, with her own headband. Jarik returned to Osyrrain. She had not gone anywhere. Sitting beside her on her firm-soft, raised bed, he showed her the dagger, hers, and then let her feel it at her throat. One-handed, he removed the cord that held the fox-tail in her mouth. Bidding her help with her tongue, he drew the long strip of sunset-colored fur from her mouth, slowly. The tail was no longer so fluffy.

Jarik gazed at her, concentrating on appearing cool, and adding some hauteur. She stared back and her brown eyes were bright. Shiny black spots in the dimness of her most private chamber.

"You may remember me. The man you whipped."

He had waited to say that until she opened her mouth

to speak. She closed it. She lay staring up at his face, as if studying him, reflecting. At last Osyrrain licked her lips, and spoke.

"You are quite the warrior indeed."

"I have defeated your god and his serpent and his guarding Pythoness, and your champion, and your bonds, Osyrrain. And I have defeated you."

"Perhaps . . . perhaps it were best. Perhaps you are the man to father the next Osyrrain."

"Ho! And if it is a boy?"

"This one is the sevent' of her line. Each of the others before this one bore a girl."

"Ah. But if you did, just perchance, bring forth a baby boy?"

"It would be slain."

Jarik nodded, a bit surprised that she had not sought to dissemble. "Osyrrain is honest. I'll not take that chance, thanks."

She showed her shock. "You refuse the Osyrrain?"

"I do," he said. "Now be silent, else I gag you very tightly indeed. If you cry out and anyone comes, I will have time—I will *take* time—to slice your mouth from one ear to the other. Think how painful, and how hideous!" After a moment he added, "Consider that a promise, and *helderen*."

She was silent. He went to look in on her servant. She was keeping nicely. Reminding Osyrrain of the virtues of silence, Jarik went to the other door. He admitted Jilain. It was she, while Osyrrain looked hatred and quivered in outrage, who found and lit a second lamp. It was carved of soapstone in the shape of a squirrel on all fours, and burned oil. Jilain struck flint and steel; again; she lit the lamp. Now Jarik took note of what a fine luxurious apartment was the Guardian of Guardians'.

"The Osyrrain lives well," he said.

Jilain had gazed for a time on her queen. Now she looked at Jarik and emotions fought each other behind her eyes. "Jarik . . ."

He picked up a beautifully woven spread, noted the

complicated, interwoven curlicues and knotwork of its pattern.

"Jarik—"

"Master weavers, your people."

She stepped before him, and her hands went onto his shoulders. Both of them, and they were warm. Eyes the color of a tawny doe looked into his sky-hued ones, and Jarik did not think her eyes resembled those of a dog.

"Jarik Blacksword."

"Jilain Kerosyris."

Her smile was without luster or, he thought, confidence. "There are hours until dawn. What will you do? Your companions were drunk, and weary. They *must* sleep. What will you do?"

He said, "Not sleep."

"No."

His eyes rolled, sending his gaze almost blandly around the chamber of the queen. His eyebrows were up ingenuously as he looked upon the woman bound half-curled on her bed. The left side of his mouth began to move. It resembled a smile. Slowly he brought his gaze back to Jilain. A sigh or agitated breath made a dully glowing ruby dance in air before her, but he would not look at it.

"What I will not do," he said, being deliberately cruel to the woman who had whipped him with her own hand, "is what Osyrrain suggested."

"No!" That from the woman lying bound on the bed.

"What's that?" Jilain asked, in complete innocence.

Osyrrain repeated, "No!"

"Be a man to her woman, perhaps to father the next Osyrrain. She has requested it."

The queen made a sob-like sound and turned her head away, mortified that he had told the other woman of her offer and of his rejection.

Jilain said, "This one has never experienced such pleasure as on that occasion years ago when she traded the whit feather for the red."

"Men feel the same," Jarik assured her. "That is why it

is so easy for the Guardians to continue doing what they do, with men. Osyrrain will have to wait for that pleasure." In his voice was only the slightest tremor.

Suddenly Jilain was looking more at his nose than into his eyes. "Wit' me, then," she said softly, and Jarik was much, much surprised.

After a time he was able to say, "No, warrior."

She blinked and compressed her lavender-hued lips, setting her teeth in the lower just a little. Her eyes now seemed to be looking at his mouth, or chin. "You see this one only as a warrior?"

He would not be so cruel as to lie to her. "No, Jilain! I see you as a woman, and I want you. I will not. I will not take the chance of leaving seed in this land. It might be a boy, who would be murdered. It might be a girl who would grow up to kidnap a lover and murder him."

Murder is only an ugly word, invented to describe a specific type of death.

She stood for a long while, looking at his chest rather than bracing his eyes, and her hands slid from his shoulders. Her own shoulders seemed to narrow.

"Must . . . must seed be spilled?"

"No. And no again, Jilain." He touched her face, touched her for the first time, and he wanted her, who wanted him. "I will not, Jilain Kerosyris. I want to possess her who hurt me, and her who was so hard to defeat. You want to be possessed by him who defeated you. I will not."

"You are . . . strong, Jarik of the Black Sword."

No, I am weak, he thought, but he would not go so far as to say so, for he was Jarik. He turned from her.

Jarik spent much of the rest of that night-into-morning forcing pleasure on Osyrrain with his hands. Giving her pleasure. Forcing her to endure pleasure. Driving her half mad with an enforced, unwanted, and perhaps unwonted ecstasy. He held himself in check, though his desire was evident to Osyrrain and to Jilain and to Jarik. Time came when he had to get up and pace while he waited for his breathing to slow.

Pacing, he noticed Jilain's back. There was almost no

central hollow and no vertebrae showed. Strange. In his curiosity, he forgot his decision not to touch her. He put his hand on her bare back while she sat at the very end corner of the Osyrrain's bed.

Jilain stiffened for a moment, before turning her head to look back and up at him, over her shoulder. Her face was open, mildly questioning. She did not smile. His hand and fingers had moved on her back.

Her vertebrae and the central depression that should have run up her back were covered by an overlay of muscle. Sheaves of muscle; a coat of muscle across her back, up and down her back, under the smooth pretty skin. Just at the turning of her head he felt that muscle move, elastic iron under the skin. He jerked back his hand.

"I am sorry. I was drawn to your back. It is so smooth. It's a strong back."

She shrugged self-consciously. "One understands. One has looked at yours. And at your breasts, too. They are rather . . . squared, and look so hard."

His smile was weak and he felt suddenly very warm of face. "Men are not said to have breasts," he told her equably, for the information. "Breast, or chest. Singular."

Yet indeed his chest was clearly divided into two halves, two bulging plates of strength with tiny nipples. She turned partway around. "Why—it is twofold, as this person's breast is. Distinctly; two halves. Breasts."

"And different," he said, feeling his face become hotter.

"Oh yes, different. And most interesting. And there's the leanness of your hips." While he remembered that he wore only his leggings, she looked abruptly down and away. "And too," she said, low, "you are so small of sitter."

He realized that was the Kerosyran term for his backside, which Lokustans called variously butt and rump and spreader, and it occurred to him fleetingly how silly it was to call it a "bottom." That word better described the feet.

"Well," Jarik said, thinking that her hands would be

good on his chest, "I am sorry I laid hand on your back, warrior."

Her head flung about again and on her face was a look of anger unto storm. For a moment she glared at him thus, and saw his surprise and lack of understanding of such a reaction. She turned away and he saw that she sat stiffly and very straight. He did not know what to do or say and so he stood doing nothing and saying nothing. And oh, the weavers were weaving. The Osyrrain heaved a great sigh and stirred amid rustling. She was ignored.

Jilain at last said, "Well, this one is not."

"You—you are not, what?"

"One is not sorry you 'laid hand on her back,'" she said, with her back to him.

"Oh."

He paced, and noted that one of the lamps contained little more oil. He paced. The prisoner's voice came petulant:

"This cord hurts one's wrists."

"Osyrrain, it will hurt as much but seem worse if I also replace your gag."

That callousness silenced her and Jarik let his pacing take him before Jilain. He said, "You could sleep, you know."

"No. One could not. You could, Jarik Blacksword."

"No," he said, "one could not." He sighed and stretched. "Will you tell me about the ruby on your breast, and the one on her forehead?" He nodded at the prisoner. Her eyes were flashing, not glowing. However ridiculous in a wark of nudity, he had thoughtfully replaced her sleeping dress over her loins.

Jilain looked as if she failed to understand his meaning and did not know how to answer. Her shrug did not make him happy, for the ruby in question seemed to flaunt itself, jumping in air before her.

"It is done," she said. "It is forever. It is what we do. Your women do not?"

He shook his head. "They also wear clothing. All of us do. At all times."

She seemed incredulous. "In summer? In the sun of high summer?"

He nodded.

"Why?"

It was his turn to look non-plussed. "It is what we do," he said. "It is often cold, in my land."

"Your land," she repeated, and looked down at nothing, idly toying with the grey-squirrel tail that was her only pretense of clothing. "In high summer?"

"No. It is warm, then. The summer is not long. But—the ruby. *How* is it forever? How is it put there? When?"

She looked up, and he watched her decide how to answer him. "For everything there must be recompense..."

"There will be recompense for you, Jilain, for this night!" the Osyrrain snapped.

Jarik's patience fled and the interruption angered him. He hurried around the bed and though she objected just short of pleading, he gagged the queen. Then he sat, and began again to force pleasure on her.

"Please tell me," he said.

Jilain had turned to face him. "With you doing *that*?"

"I shall stop." He did and ignored Osyrrain's gasping. "The rubies, worn so, are not like anything I have ever seen or heard of."

"Oh. Nor has one ever seen or heard of hair like that on the one called Delak—white, but not with age. Yours is as pale as any this one has ever seen, and that not often."

"Delath. Yes. About recompense..."

"You must know," Jilain said. "For how can truths differ from land to land?—From your land to this? For all things there must be recompense."

"Payment," he suggested, nodding.

"Sometimes it is long in coming. For the Guardians, there is this sign of the Guardian. The—" And she used a word he did not know. Lankit? Llanket? or Lanketh, perhaps? He was not sure; the word was new, and belonged only to Kerosyr. Having said that word, Jilain touched her breast and continued:

"It is the badge of the Guardian, and all on Osyr's island are Guardians. Girls look forward to it. We receive it when we have lived twelve years or are in our twelfth year on the day of Lainosyra, in spring. That day a girl becomes a Guardian, and she is proud and stands tall. Yet there must be recompense. In pain, then, we receive the Llanket. As, on her ascension, the Osyrrain receives Osyr's sign on her forehead in pain. The pain does not last. Occasionally some are ill afterward, but not for long. A girl died once—in this one's lifetime, one means; there have been others. For some reason Osyr rejected her and she died and we were sad." Jilain made a gesture. "It brings no pain after, ever again. Unless the Moon-Mother has not been perfect or Osyr demands more recompense. In those times the skin starts to grow over the Llanket. It must be removed."

"The skin."

"Yes."

"How is it done? How comes the pain?"

"Oh. The gems are bonded to the flesh by being held against it while the gem is smoking hot. It . . . sizzles. That way, it is part of the flesh, part of the Guardian. It is permanent." And with her fingernails she tapped her own Llanket.

Jarik, who was circumcised, thought that what he heard was terrible, ridiculous; barbaric. He did not say so, though he made a face. He wondered how large the world was, and how many strange people and customs were in it. It would be interesting to find out, he thought. Perhaps, once he had returned—if he did—and slain milady Snowmist—if he could—as he had agreed to do for the Iron Lords; perhaps then he and the Lords of Iron could discuss things he might do. Missions he might perform that would take him to other places of other peoples. No more all-women societies, he hoped. And . . . action. He should be happy to experience more of the sword-reddening action. Jarik enjoyed it. Jarik enjoyed combat, when he was so vehemently alive and could be sure, absolutely sure, that he was gloriously competent. More than competent!

'*Nice*' *or not*, he thought, *I enjoy fighting, spilling blood... I enjoy killing.*

"Jarik Blacksword?"

He looked at her.

"You said that you wished this one's name was— something else. Jileeyee?"

He sighed. "Jilye," he corrected. "Or Jilyish. Yes, I said that."

"Why? It is still this one's name?"

"Here, all names end in the *-ain* sound."

"Not until one receives the Llanket, and is Guardian," she told him.

"In my land, female names end in *-ye*. The more familiar, the..." He looked away. "The family form or fondness form for both males and females, is to end a name in *-ish*. I was 'Jarish' to my Family, and... and those fond of me. Jilye becomes Jilyish."

"*Oh.*"

She said that very softly, and her eyes had gone soft, looking at him. She understood now what he had meant before, what he had been saying. He wished that she were of his people. Not... an enemy. And Jilain of Kerosyr looked away. She was too affected to ask the question that had occurred to her: What is 'family'?

Jerkily then, ignoring the fact that he wished it were Jilain, Jarik put his hand on Osyrrain. Cruelly, perversely, as if compulsively, he returned to forcing pleasure on the Guardian of Guardians. And she writhed. Jilain looked away.

Though Osyrrain was made to know happiness or at least ecstasy—which was not the same,—in a mechanical sort of way, none of the three knew happiness that night. Jarik, in the presence of a warrior and a woman he respected and desired, would not act on the desire. Jilain, in the presence of a warrior and a man she could respect, she who had been once with a man and enjoyed it so that she had not quite been happy since, could do nothing about her respect and desire for him. Osyrrain was made to weep, with a surfeit of displaced pleasure. It was demeaning. So Jarik intended it to be. He punished Osyrrain while punishing Jilain while punishing Jarik.

Too, he explained to them his plan for tomorrow. Jilain made suggestions that improved it. She asked too about other gods, and about his bracers. Jarik told her some things and withheld some. Desire and lack of sleep gave him a headache that he never mentioned.

The night was long. When outside sounds assured them that dawn had come, all three were more than ready for the new day. Jarik told Jilain that it was time, and they looked long at each other. Then Jilain rose and left the chamber.

She soon returned with two Guardians, hunter-warriors. She made them wait just outside the door of the inner chamber. To its left against the inside wall stood Jarik, so that he was not visible to Jilain's squad of two. Osyrrain lay nicely covered on her bed, and her mouth was free. She understood that if she gave the situation away, her Guardians would naturally be a bit slower to react than Jarik—who would be upon her.

So that the others could hear, the queen bade Jilain fetch here the leader of the invaders, and rouse the others.

"The leader?" A Guardian asked. "That Jarik?"

"No," Osyrrain said petulantly, her gaze straying to the flash of her own eating knife in Jarik's grasp. "He of the one arm."

"As the Osyrrain wishes," Jilain said, and the trio departed.

"The Osyrrain is wise," Jarik said.

"And prisoner, and weary, and sore, and demeaned—and hungry!"

"But not," Jarik said, "whipped, or sore of back."

She jerked her face aside to stare at a wall, and quite

soon Jilain brought Kirrensark who looked dull.

He became alert while Jarik apprised him of their situation and the fate reserved for the Lokustans if they did not depart sooner. The while, outside, news spread rapidly. The Osyrrain, abed, had sent for the big one-armed leader of the men. Women rolled eyes, grinned or smirked, made faces. Soon, they assumed, their queen would wear the red feather. Good! It was time. She was a full score of years old, and *so* austere and proud.

They watched Jilain and Kirrensark emerge from the Osyrrain-house. They went to that disguised greathouse that was actually a cushioned, silken prison.

Full of muttering and smiles and gossip, the village went distractedly about its business. Work was disrupted and silence fell again when Jilain and her two warriors returned. They escorted all the men who had come yesterday. All! Jokes were made and remarks were called out, not by men.

"Cease this noise!" Jilain called sharply. "Much food and drink is required by the Osyrrain!"

"Much indeed," someone muttered, and "So many men," someone else muttered, and there was giggling. "More dough!" a more practical woman cracked. "More milk! Hurry it along."

Watching women and girls did little save watch, however, while all those males entered the house of the Osyrrain. The Guardians looked at each other. Brows rose and eyes rolled. Some had enjoyed their experience with a man. Some had not or were ambivalent. The ruler must belong in the company of the former. A busy, excited murmur rose and hummed around the village like a swarm of insects. Food and drink were gathered and prepared for the Osyrrain and her *guests*—in quantity.

Bearers of food were not admitted to the innermost chamber, and returned to disappoint their questioning comrades. The Guardians could only speculate. They speculated.

Within, Jarik made explanation to grumbling,

headachy men of Lokusta, who looked on women this day with a remarkably low interest. Jilain, meanwhile, returned outside. She answered no questions. She directed that the men's armor, shields, helms and weapons be gathered before the Osyrrain-house. Jilain did not seem happy, and was peevish. But then she was a moody strangel anyhow.

It was the Moon-Mother who questioned the instructions.

Jilain returned to her, noting that the Moon-Mother wore the Black Sword. "This one does not question the Osyrrain," she said, with only a hint of asperity. "It is the Osyrrain's wish and desire." And with the briefest of ritual inclinations of her head, she returned within the big building. The men's possessions were collected and carried there as she had instructed.

Jilain, meanwhile, was advising Jarik that all save two of those women, who today were red feather for the first time, were exquisitely happy. Rolling eyes at the queen, she added, "As was this one when she changed feathers."

"And where is that man," a very grim Delath Berserker asked, "who gave you such happiness?"

Jilain turned away without answering.

"Enough of that," Jarik said. "Let there be no such questions, which are accusations and serve us no purpose. Our concern is to be away from here, and in peace. Nor will I ask which two of the new red-feather Guardians are *not* happy this day! Eat. Ignore the throbbing in your swollen heads, you gluttons, you sated bulls! I, Jarik, have saved you all."

As soon as he had said that, Jarik and Jilain looked at each other. Only their eyes spoke.

Osyrrain's bound servant had long since been removed from the adjoining room, and untied. She huddled near her mistress, overawed. Now she and Jilain accompanied the Osyrrain into that chamber, that the queen might prepare herself free of the gaze of men. They heard her castigating Jilain.

"Did you have that bitch, Jarik?"

"What do you think?"

Several men chuckled. Tole did not. "I think we should kill them all, these monsters in female form!"

"You may be right," Jarik said quietly. "Consider that it is their land, though. They know the forest and are at home in it as you are in your own garden. And make no mistake: They are superb with those bone-plated bows of theirs. Still, I would say that we could kill many of them, before they slew us all."

Many looked at Jarik then, and at Tole, who stood blinking. He made a face and turned away muttering. Delath, who was old enough to have fathered Jarik— provided he had done so at a perfectly normal seventeen or so—gazed upon Jarik. Slowly, reluctantly, he nodded. It was then the three women emerged from the small adjoining chamber. Osyrrain walked with her head high and her feathers in place. She carried herself as the ruler she was, and would not look at Jarik.

The plan was laid, and continued. Without her weapons, Jilain went out to make the awesome announcement: the Osyrrain was prisoner of the men, who would not harm her provided they were allowed to return to their ship and depart. After the first exclamations and murmurous comments, there fell the silence of shock. Then Ershain spoke loud.

"If we let them leave, they may return with more and kill us all!"

Jilain nodded. "We shall have to set watches on the coast after this, and arrange more defenses. We are hardly easy prey, Ershain."

"But—why not slay them all now?"

"They have the Osyrrain. Will you move against one of them, knowing that she dies on the instant?"

No. "Was—was it she who brought this on? In her sudden greed for men?"

"You answer, Ershain. It was not this one who called all those men to her chamber!"

No one laughed. Though none liked it, two men emerged. They moved only far enough from the doorway of the Osyrrain-house to gather arms and armor. They conveyed it within, and returned for more, and vanished inside. The Guardians forgot or forsook all else, and stood staring at the Osyrrain-house. Men were arming themselves, within the wark!

Jarik came forth. Many eyes stared at him and the scintillant flash of his coat of chain. He could almost feel the hatred behind those brown eyes, the itch and ache to attack. It would be easy for them, he knew. He had seen their skill at archery. His own sword-sheath hung empty at his side. He wore his dagger, handed him again by Jilain.

"We have no wish to hurt anyone," he called. "We return to our ship and that is our only desire. We take Osyrrain with us, only as far as the shore. She will be in our midst, well surrounded. I do not *want* to hurt her, Guardians of Osyr. This one is Jarik, and he knows that your promises are sacred and unbreakable. You know that those of men are not. I tell you, Guardians of Osyr, that this promise of mine is. We will not harm Osyrrain, or any of you . . . provided you let us go from among you. Try to prevent that, or harm us or one of us—and she will surely die. So, surely, will many of you."

"And many of you!" a woman shouted.

Jarik nodded. "Of course," he said.

In silence, blue-haired women glared. The silence was human only; birds whistled and trilled, and insects chirred. Eyes glared. Jarik met the dog-tawny eyes of Ershain. She stared. Behind him inside, Jarik knew, Kirrensark was warning his men while they busked. They were to walk through the forest and to the shore. Down the beach and to the ship. Onto the ship. They were not to provoke or respond to provocation.

"We must agree!"

The dry yet ringing voice was that of her called the Moon-Mother. She stepped before the others, and turned to address them. Jarik recognized the red-wrapped hilt of the sword sheathed at her side. She had made it part of her garb and her authority, had she? A thought struck him and he had to avoid smiling.

"We must agree, and let these *men* go! We cannot suffer them to slay the Osyrrain! They stay alive by keeping her alive; we keep her alive by letting them go. We cannot give them cause to lay about among us, now they have their weapons and their coats of metal and hard leather. We must agree!"

She turned to fix Jarik with her gaze, this one respected woman among the Guardians who wore clothing. "The Guardians will be all about you as you trek through *our* wood, *man*. Quivers will be full and bows strung. Do you understand?"

"I understand, beloved of Osyr. My companions are instructed to say nothing and do naught but walk. I hope no one tests them too sorely. We wish to do nothing to cause arrows to be loosed upon us."

"Then the Guardians shall loose none!"

After her eyes had roasted him for a moment longer she whirled again to face the gathered people of Kerosyr. Females of all ages; all, all females. A feather, a necklace of shells and dangling mousehide bag, a braided leather strand about the hips. Daggers on most and swords on some. Some with squirrel or fox tails pendent between their upper thighs. All with blue hair and lavender lips, and the llanket.

Jarik waited until he thought the Moon-Mother must be opening her mouth to address them further.

"I would have my Black Sword," he said. "It is a sword of gods, the Black Sword of the Iron Lords who are great gods, and alive. It is my Sword, and I would have it."

The mailed blond standing before the Osyrrain-house put forth a hand. Twenty paces away, the Moon-Mother stiffened. Automatically her hand moved toward the hilt at her side; automatically she jerked that hand away with a gasp, *for the hilt was moving*, upward. While all the

wark watched, the Black Sword, untouched, left the
sheath she had donned to contain it. The Sword had
drawn itself. It hovered for a moment in air, a naked,
black-bladed sword touched by no hand, afloat in air. Yet
not merely afloat, for it was sentient or seemed so.

It tipped, tilted to the horizontal, point toward the
Guardians. Then it rushed to Jarik, hilt-foremost. The
Guardians were silently aware that they witnessed
sorcery; that the hand of a god must indeed be upon this
man; that he must indeed have power. Jarik's hand closed
on the hilt he had tightly wrapped with red leather to
disguise its strange unrefulgent hilt and undistinguished
pommel.

His fist closed one the Black Sword of the Iron Lords.
He lifted it high, in fine drama. Then he thrust it home
into its sheath.

The Moon-Mother had been forced to turn and stare.
Now, slowly, reasserting her self control, she turned back
to gathered Kerosyr. To whom Jarik, carefully, deliberately, had displayed what he knew they would take as
power.

"The Osyrrain is captive," the Moon-Mother said, and
Jarik was pleased at the momentary quaver in her voice.
"I speak for her. I speak for the *god*. Ershain: choose three
tens of archers. All will wear full quivers and carry their
bows *strung*. All are to accompany the men to the strand,
to their craft—and without speaking." She scanned them
slowly, letting them feel her gaze. "Hear and understand.
Speak no taunts. *No arrow must be loosed*. No man must
be touched. I speak for the god."

Perhaps, Jarik mused. He wondered what Osyr might
say for himself, were he more than a statue of black stone
and a Guide in dreams. After a moment he realized that it
was done. They were committed. They had agreed. Jarik
turned and went back into the greathouse, to fetch his
companions and their hostage.

13

The Honor of Osyr

"The wrong use of a thing is far worse than the non-use.
——Socrates

"...but the contrary of an evil is sometimes a good, sometimes an evil.

——Aristotle

They walked in tension thick and palpable as that which precedes a violent storm. The air was heavy with it. Even the forest seemed aware, and was still. Guardian women, and the male invaders who enveloped and surrounded Osyrrain; the Osyrrain of Osyr. No one spoke. Men walked carefully in their buskins, mindful of their steps and of each other. Leather creaked. Chain links rustled and occasionally clinked. The Guardians, bare of feet, glided lightly and noiselessly, moving only below the hips without seeming to take note of where they trod. Naked or nearly, and each with a precious blood-hued gemstone bonded to her flesh.

Jarik had deemed it wise to wrap the god's ivory rod in cloth, and to let another man bear it casually, that attention might not be drawn to what they took with them. This he had soon effected, and he had no real notion how happy and important he made young Coon feel.

Wiser than he counted himself, Jarik elected to leave behind the golden chain from the temple. It was not a thing to be flaunted as spoils.

Tension ruled now. Its setting was a maze of leafy branches, cones and needles forming a strange formless design against the cerulean background that was the sky. Even birds seemed muted in their fluttering and calling, their warbling and skittering. The myriad tiny creatures of the forest ceased their chitter and whistling sounds when the humans approached. The wood seemed to hold its breath while they trod past, all in silence. The forest floor, bare nowhere, crackled and whished and popped beneath their feet. Little coppery gleams were bits of husk, all that enterprising squirrels had left of acorns.

Armed, armored men, moving through the woods, *away* from the village of the Guardians of Osyr. Others had come this way, toward the village; were these the first to depart? Jarik wondered. He smelled pine cones—thick, faintly metallic—and the moulder underfoot—rich, nascently sourish—and he was aware of the smell of *green*. And . . . of tension. Aye, it had an odor, tension did. And it could be felt.

The band of men paced with Osyrrain at its center. Beside her was Jarik of the Black Sword. At their head was Kirrensark One-arm. First man of Kirrensark-wark. Leader and yet not leader. Was Jarik leader?

No. All of this was commanded, presided over by the *god* afar. Not dead Osyr, but living; the Lady of the Snowmist.

Before and behind glided women. Naked women; the Guardians. Erect and moveless from the hips up. Feathers nodding above their heads. Quivers full. Horn-plated bows tautly strung. More of them paced the cavalcade on either side, out of sight, and every man knew it.

Jarik wore helm and mailcoat and the Black Sword. Sweat hurt his back. He could not pay attention.

An odor of forest, of pungent herbs encircled them all in an aromatic wreath, and so did the smell of fear, and of

tension. They moved in silence disrupted only by an
occasional male curse. Though naked, the Guardians did
not seem troubled by these plaguey insects. Enemies:
men, and women. Enemies. Jarik marched with the men,
and now and again his arm touched that of Osyrrain.
Jilain paced with the women. Their eyes did not meet,
hers and Jarik's, though each thought of the others. Each
was emphatically aware of the other.

Nor did Jarik think *I bested her.* Instead he reflected
that she had fought him superbly, that he respected
her—that he wanted her. Never did he think on those
words the Guide had last said to him: *A part of you is a
tree, and a part of you is a woman, and two parts of you lie
on an island, close to union . . . when you are whole—
three as one . . .*

Who knew what Jilain thought?

None knew that she had freed him, who was Osyrrain's
intended victim of this day. She *did* think, she who had
said that her greatest occasion of pleasure had come when
years ago she had been with a man. A man now dead. She
had said she was not happy. Did she question such a
culture? Did she know that in other lands conquerors
often took their pleasure of women, and then slew them?
Did she even dream of other lands? Jilain moved with the
Guardians. Gliding with her bow and with a ruby bonded
to her breast, the tail of a grey squirrel aswing between her
thighs, red feather erect above her blue hair, and she did
much thinking. And the weavers were weaving.

No incident marred the trek. The peace was kept.

They came to the edge of the forest. Bright light shrank
their pupils and they gazed blinking upon the long bright
strand that slanted down to the sea. And there was
Seadancer, waiting. Kirrensark paused, who had been
Kirrensark Long-haft, hawker. Now he fled women, and
a gloomy yunker commanded more than he. On the
service of Her.

After the pause of a moment he continued walking.

Down the strand toward the long boat called ship. Behind him the leaves of trees commenced to rustle, and the feathers trembled above blue-haired heads. The breeze had risen of a sudden, and it blew directly out to sea.

"Guardians halt!" Jarik shouted, into silence. He stood beside Osyrrain and all around him were mailed, armed men with sunlight in their helmets.

Kirrensark halted and wheeled, ten paces ahead of the others, alone. *"Guardians Halt!"* he bawled, for he was firstman and ship's master.

The Guardians glanced at the men, at each other, and paused. They did not look halted; their sinuous bodies represented motion arrested temporarily.

"Guardians halt here!" Osyrrain called.

Her people came to their individual halts, then. More Guardians came from the forest, and they stopped. And more came, and stopped there, at wood's edge. Thirty-one women with full quivers and taut-strung bows held not idly in the left hand. A thirty-second was the queen's champion, who had never been defeated since her thirteenth summer. Until yesterday. Her quiver was on her hip; her bow was on her back. She wore sword and dagger, and the barely adequate skin of a grey squirrel, its tail dangling between her thighs.

"To the ship," Kirrensark said, and turned and walked. Behind his broad back were thirty-one bows and surely over three hundred striped arrows.

Men moved past Jarik and Osyrrain, looked at Jarik. He nodded. The queen looked at him. The men moved on. Buskins scuffed and crunched on sand. They followed their firstman down the beach to *Seadancer*. The ship was hale and ready. They set stocky legs and put their backs to it, and pushed her down into the surf. Women looked from them to Jarik and their ruler, who had paced twenty steps along the beach. Twenty steps behind were the Guardians, and thirty bows; thirty-two, for there were Ershain's and Jilain's. Forty paces ahead was *Seadancer*.

Her fellows watched Jilain, then, while she paced to a point a little nearer Osyrrain, nearer Jarik. But her hands remained empty.

Jarik looked at the one man who remained, standing on the other side of the queen. He looked at Jarik, and he remained behind while the others floated *Seadancer* in a lively surf and began mounting her. A breeze blew from the woods, out to sea. The remaining man was Delath Morbriner. White-blond hair fluttered below his helm.

"Delath," Jarik said.

"I am here."

"Go with the others."

"You do not command, Jarik Blacksword. I go when you go."

The two men looked at each other. Morbrin-fighters both: *machines-that-fight*; they who fight as the wolf fights. Warriors; not friends. Yet Delath chose to remain with Jarik, in danger. Respect for courage superceded antipathy.

"I remain to hold the Osyrrain, Delath Berserker."

"With many arrows behind you. And when you let go her?"

"I will join you on the ship."

"I go when you go, Jarik Blacksword."

The two men looked at each other.

"Go," Osyrrain said. "We will not seek to stop you now."

The others were aboard *Seadancer*. She was afloat and restless. They stared back at the beach of Kerosyr. At Jarik, at thirty-two bow-armed Guardians, at Delath of the pale, pale beard: no admirer of Jarik's and longtime friend of Kirrensark. Jarik stood very close to the queen, and held her arm. On her other side, Delath did not touch her.

"Say that again, Osyrrain," Jarik said. "Very loudly."

She looked at him, as Delath looked at her, and she repeated her words. Loudly, for her women. "Go! We will not seek to stop you now!"

"At rest," Ershain said, not quite as loudly. "Let them go as the Osyrrain commands."

Jarik stepped away from Osyrrain, turned. "We leave you, Guardians," he said, and all heard. "Remove yourselves backward, to the very edge of the trees."

"Do not seek to take her, Jarik!"

He let his gaze meet Ershain's, and he nodded. "She remains, Ershain. I have promised it."

Ershain made a little sound and the Guardians backed, to the very edge of the treeline. The very air seemed heavy. Jarik was sweating. Bird-songs were intrusions. Kirrensark alone had not boarded his ship, but waited near *Seadancer*, behaving as a first man should. All of his but two were aboard his ship, and the tension had not abated a whit.

"Farewell, Osyrrain," Jarik muttered, and looked past her for he expected no reply. "Delath."

Jarik looked at the ship. His back prickled. Sweat trickled and was fire in the whip-weals on his back, under mail and jack and tunic.

"When you are ready, Jarik Blacksword."

Jarik glanced at the other man. "I am ready. Go!"

Delath's gaze was very steady. "When you let go this queen of murderers and go, Jarik Blacksword. Then goes Delath called Morbriner."

"Delath . . . we have given our word." When he'd said that, Jarik felt Osyrrain tense. "*Kiddensok!*" Jarik called. "Delath!"

Kirrensark, dutifully, called, "Delath! Board ship!"

Delath looked back at thirty-two bow-armed Guardians, and at Osyrrain, and at Jarik. And he took his hand from his hilt. Delath *backed* down the strand, and Jarik knew Osyrrain seethed, insulted. Delath allowed Shranshule to aid him aboard the ship. He turned at once, watchful, showing his distrust. Pale eyes above pale beard, and eyebrows no darker than the sand of the beach.

Jarik took a deep breath. He scanned the beach ahead

of him and saw no obstruction or depression to turn an ankle. He let go Osyrrain's arm. Then Jarik raced to the waterline, his mailcoat jingling and his back all aprickle. Behind him, just as his feet splashed for the first time, he heard the shout. The voice was Osyrrain's, and Jarik went cold.

"SLAY THEM!"

"Bows!" Delath yelled. "Up bows for Kirrensark!"

"No!" Jarik called, and he clamped his lips and splashed dodgily through the water while his back crawled. He reached the ship. For an instant he and Kirrensark looked each into the eyes of the other. Jarik looked back to see women frowning, eyes rolling; to see arrows being moved slowly, uncertainly from quivers toward taut bowstrings—and one of Osyr's Guardians leaping, ahead of the others. Almost naked, jiggling as other women jiggle, she raced and her sword was out in her hand. She ran toward the Osyrrain. She was reaching the Osyrrain...

As she passed, at the run, that Guardian struck. Racing, bosses flashing on her leather helm, shell necklace and squirrel-tail crotchpiece wildly amove, she struck. With one sweep of her blade, that one Guardian accomplished the incredible: she beheaded the Osyrrain. No hair covered that queenly neck, and the sword was sharp and well swung, backed with the momentum of the Guardian's racing pace. The head flew on a wake of scarlet, and struck the sparkling sand, and rolled. The eyes glared and flashed bright as gemstones.

All froze, staring, but one. She continued running, down the strand until she was splashing in water, and she was at Jarik's side beneath *Seadancer*'s fierce hawk-head prow. And his bracers were not cold. Beside him, she turned.

"The Osyrrain gave an Osyrrain's promise!" she shouted, and her voice hurt Jarik's ears. "And she spoke too for Osyr! The men know not the helderen-promise— and yet they *kept* theirs! Would you allow a promise to be

helderen only until the Osyrrain decides on treachery?
Would you allow her to rob Osyr of honor, because she
had none? Guardians! Choose now an *honorable* ruler!"

She whirled then, and reached up to the ship. As she
stretched, Kirrensark came alive; he seized her thighs and
lifted her. Two hands reached down, and they were
Delath's. Dripping, the Guardian of Osyr turned her
naked backside to her people, and to the sun, and
scrambled aboard *Seadancer*. Whirling at once, she
reached down for Jarik of the Black Sword.

She aided him aboard while two others drew up
Kirrensark, while still those on shore stood staring,
shocked into immobility with their bows and their arrows
in their hands. First the dilemma of whether to break a
queen's promise, because she wanted revenge. And now
dilemma continued: break a queen's helderen promise to
avenge that queen in her death?

Their blue hair stirred for the wind was blowing and
the sail was up and all the same Kirrensark was hardly
aboard before he bawled, "ROW!"

Seadancer moved. The weavers wove while gods
plotted and strove, and thus did Jilain Kerosyris join
forces with Jarik Blacksword and with the forces of the
Lady of the Snowmist, in the war among the gods on the
earth.

**This was
the second
of the chronicles
of
Jarik and Jilain
in
The War Among the Gods on the Earth**